Front Runner

A Political Thriller

by

Frederick Gooltz

Front Runner

A Political Thriller

Copyright © 2024 Fred Gooltz

Lunavox Unlimited

DEDICATION

This story would not be possible without the assistance of Maggie Moon. Additional thanks to Justin Krebs, Matt O'Neill, and Katrina Baker who got me so interested in politics that it became my vocation for a time. The adventures that I had on our political campaigns informed these pages.

Author's Note

My experience as a political strategist and speechwriter in Washington D.C. compelled me to change some of the names …for secret reasons.

\- F.G.

FRONT RUNNER

TEASER

The blue siren lights of the Georgia State Police squad car spun in hypnotic circles, casting eerie flashes across the brick façade of Southern Village Marketplace Mall. The vehicle sat at an angle, deliberately blocking the tree-lined driveway into the new shopping center-office park. Beyond this impromptu barricade lay a picturesque suburban commercial complex, its architecture designed to evoke small-town charm despite its reality.

From above, the scene resembled a meticulously arranged model town. A quaint oval-shaped Village Green formed the heart of the complex, complete with a white gazebo standing proudly at its center. Surrounding this patch of carefully maintained lawn, building blocks of artisanal stores and trendy cafés circled like wagons around a campfire. Office spaces occupied the second floors, while a select few residential suites perched above everything else, offering their occupants a bird's-eye view of the community below.

The clock tower anchoring the main building commanded attention, rising above the surrounding structures like a watchful sentinel. Inside its windowed face, a blur of movement caught the eye—a figure sprinting past, desperation radiating from every step.

Inside the clock tower, the pounding of feet echoed against the enclosed stairwell. Tight jeans and green Converse All-Stars hit the stairs with determined force, taking them two at a time in a frantic ascent. Lyric Zumwalt, thirty years old and running for her life, gasped for breath as sweat beaded across her flushed face. Panic surged through her veins like electricity, propelling her upward despite the burning in her thighs.

She paused momentarily, hands gripping the stair railing as she leaned over to peer down. The spiral of stairs below revealed her pursuers—state cops in uniform, moving with methodical determination, gaining ground with each passing second. Their footfalls echoed in the confined space, a drumbeat of approaching consequences.

A surge of adrenaline pushed her onward. Reaching the next landing, Lyric pressed her face to a small window, her breath fogging the glass as she surveyed the scene below--

Outside, on the Village Green driveway, additional gray state police cruisers pulled up in formation, screeching to a halt in front of the main building. Car doors kicked open in unison, and officers emerged with practiced efficiency. One officer raised a bullhorn to his mouth, his voice booming across the otherwise peaceful shopping center.

"Turn yourself in!" The amplified command bounced off brick walls and storefront windows.

Another officer took a defensive position, kneeling behind his open car door with his rifle at the ready, the barrel poking through the open window. His stance spoke of years of training, of situations where lives hung in the balance.

Lyric continued her racing ascent, legs screaming in protest as she reached the final flight of stairs. Above her the empty decorative belfry beckoned, awash in bright daylight streaming through its open architecture. The realization struck her with crushing weight—she'd reached a dead end. There was nowhere left to run.

"Don't jump! Hands up!" The voices of the state police officers closing in from behind carried an edge of both authority and caution.

Desperation clawed at her insides as Lyric yanked at the window, attempting to force it open, to find any escape route. The light from outside blazed almost blindingly bright, disorienting her as she spun around to face her pursuers. The state police officers burst onto the landing, their shouts piercing the air as they screamed commands directly at her, their faces contorted with intensity.

The world froze in that moment—suspended between what was and what would come next. How had all this nightmare started?

FRIDAY

Fifty-two hours earlier, fluorescent lights hummed overhead in a cluttered basement storage room in Washington D.C. Lyric sat at a small table surrounded by advocacy literature—flyers and poster-boards bearing the "Parks1" logo, a local parks advocacy organization operating within the nation's capital.

The harsh lighting cast unflattering shadows across her face as she methodically matched entries in a bank deposit book against data displayed on her laptop screen. For hours, she'd been cross-referencing numbers, fact-checking with meticulous attention to detail. Her finger traced along a row of figures, stopping at yet another perfect match. A small smile of satisfaction crossed her lips as she stood and gathered her belongings.

Behind her, a Parks1 intern—barely twenty and clearly bored with his assignment—slept soundly in a corner chair. He'd been tasked with watching Lyric as she examined his organization's financial records, but exhaustion had evidently won out over responsibility.

Not wanting to embarrass him, Lyric closed the copy machine lid with deliberate force, the thump loud enough to disturb his slumber without seeming intentional. She added a polite cough for good measure, granting him the dignity of believing he'd woken on his own.

K Street lay quiet under the pre-dawn sky as the intern, grumpy from his interrupted nap, unlocked the door to let Lyric out of his building.

"Sorry you had to babysi—" Lyric began, her tone genuinely apologetic.

The door slammed shut before she could finish, cutting off her words mid-sentence. Unfazed by the rudeness, she looped her scarf around her neck against the bite of D.C.'s autumn air. Her fingers, slightly numb from the cold, pulled her phone from her pocket and dialed a number from her "recent calls." She moved with purpose, her pace quickening with each step.

"I need Tae-sung," she spoke into the phone, her breath forming small clouds in the chilly air. "All done; They're clean, the story is bullshit." She paused, listening to the response on the other end. A wave of disgust hit her face. "You at the office - I'm coming in. Hold the story! I'm coming!"

Her brisk walk burst into a determined run, her green Converse All-Stars striking against the pavement in a steady rhythm as she raced toward her destination.

* * *

The Washington Journal's elevator doors slid to a close as Lyric narrowly slipped inside. Her newspaper's logo, a testament to former journalistic integrity, glowed into the lobby from the wall. It was a reminder of the weight her words carried, of the responsibility that came with safeguarding the truth.

Lyric burst into her desk editor's office, her eyes immediately locking onto her boss, Tae-sung Lee. The 47-year-old editor stood with a look of resigned frustration, accompanied by a smug journalist whose hand was extended to Lyric in an offer of introduction.

"Tae, you can't print that story. It's a hit-piece on Senator Nordström with NO evidence. I checked the books." Her voice carried the conviction of someone who'd done their homework, who stood on solid factual ground.

Only after making her point did Lyric turn to acknowledge the waiting journalist, belatedly accepting his handshake.

"Hi, I'm not calling you a liar—you were lied to, you should be mad." She directed her gaze back to Tae-sung. "Tae, I fact-checked every org. Senator Nordström is not buying endorsements—"

"Lyric." Tae-sung's interruption carried a warning. "There are important people who want this story printed."

She squared her shoulders, indignation flaring in her eyes. "So what!? I don't care if his source is important. They're planting a lie. And we have a responsibility—"

"Our. Boss." Tae-sung emphasized each word separately. "...is who wants this."

Lyric planted her feet more firmly, as if physically bracing herself against this revelation. She swung her saddle bag from her shoulder.

"Here, we 'comfort the afflicted and afflict the comfortable,' you said." Her tone carried the bite of betrayal, throwing his own words back at him.

"Is it possible that—" he began, searching for middle ground.

"No." Lyric cut him off. "I literally have all the budgets!"

With dramatic finality, she extracted a thick stack of photocopied ledger pages from her bag and dropped them onto Tae-sung's desk with a resounding thud. The sound punctuated her point more effectively than any additional words could have.

Tae-sung's expression revealed conflicting emotions—pride in her thoroughness mingled with irritation at the complication she'd introduced.

"Lyric, you can go. Thanks..." He exhaled heavily. "Go home."

She remained rooted in place, her glare shifting to the journalist, clearly expecting her boss to reprimand him as well. The unspoken accusation hung in the air between them.

"We have to discuss his source. Sleep." Tae-sung's tone softened slightly, but remained firm.

Reluctantly, Lyric gathered her bag and headed for the door. As she left the two men to their discussion, doubt clung to her like a shadow. Despite her evidence, despite the truth she'd uncovered through hours of diligent work, she lacked confidence the newspaper—her newspaper—would choose integrity over influence.

The door closed behind her with a soft click, but the questions remained. In a world where power dictated narrative, what value did truth truly hold?

* * *

Morning light streamed through the smudged windows of a cramped corner bodega deli. Lyric stood at a window counter, mechanically consuming a breakfast sandwich, her mind still replaying the confrontation with Tae-sung. The scent of coffee and toast permeated the small space, mingling with the sharp tang of floor cleaner drying in some aisle behind her.

Her phone buzzed against the counter, its screen illuminating with a text notification from "DAVID P." Immediate annoyance flashed across her face, her jaw tightening as she recognized the name. David—her former coworker whose inappropriate advances had persisted long after she'd made her disinterest clear.

Lyric! Where are you!?

She rolled her eyes, a low grumble escaping her throat. Opening the message chain, she scrolled backward through months of one-sided conversations—his persistent texts met with her consistent silence. The sheer volume of unanswered messages spoke to his inability to take a hint.

Chewing thoughtfully, she considered what response might finally end this unwanted attention. Her fingers hovered over the screen before typing:

Worked all night. No end in sight.

His response arrived almost instantly, as if he'd been clutching his phone, waiting to paste it:

I miss our late night sessions ;)

The winking emoji sent a shiver of disgust through Lyric. Her face contorted in revulsion, sandwich momentarily forgotten.

"I'm not flirting, dude. Jesus," she muttered to the empty air beside her. Her thumbs jabbed at the screen with renewed irritation.

Behave.

The single word carried the weight of her exasperation. Before she could set the phone down, it began to ring— "DAVID P" flashing on the screen. With a sharp exhale, Lyric answered, pressing the phone against her ear.

"What!" she snapped, abandoning any pretense of politeness. Her expression shifted from annoyance to confusion as she listened. "*Specifically* I live in DC, why!?" Her eyes narrowed in suspicion. "I'm a few blocks away, why??"

The combative edge in her voice gave way to perplexed curiosity, sandwich abandoned on its greasy paper wrapping.

***

Lyric walked around the corner onto her street, the phone still pressed to her ear. Her eyes widened as she spotted a sleek black SUV parked in front of her dilapidated apartment building. The crisply-suited driver, looking comically out of place in her rundown neighborhood, held a sign with her name—"Lyric Zumwalt"—as if she were a dignitary arriving at an international terminal.

The phone still pressed to her ear, she continued her bewildered conversation with David.

"David, I told you, I like my job!" Her free hand gestured emphatically as she spoke. "Fact-checking is important too…" She paused, listening to his response. "OK. Fine, one meeting…" Her voice rose in pitch and volume. "Private jet?"

The driver caught her eye and nodded with an exaggerated waggle of his eyebrows, confirming the extravagance awaiting her.

The journey unfolded like a surreal dream: the black SUV gliding through Washington traffic to National Airport's exclusive private terminal; Lyric ascending the steps to a sleek, pearl-white jet; her slim fingers wrapped around a crystal glass of amber champagne as she sat alone in the luxurious cabin; the aircraft descending through cotton-like clouds, its wheels contacting the runway in a brief, skipping impact.

When the wheels hit the tarmac with a jolt, Lyric startled awake, momentarily disoriented. She blinked rapidly, trying to reconcile her surroundings with the world she'd left behind mere hours ago.

***

The tiny terminal of the north Georgia private airport shimmered with an air of efficiency reserved for the elite. Lyric exited the glass door into the daylight, dragging her luggage behind her like an anchor to reality.

A sweet African American driver with graying hair waved, his warm smile a most welcome sight.

"Miss Lyric? Can I take your bag? I'm Ty. I'll take care'a you today."

Lyric returned his greeting with a grateful nod, gesturing for him to lead the way. The formality of the situation—the private jet, the personal driver—hung awkwardly around her shoulders like an ill-fitting coat.

Inside another black SUV—this one somehow more imposing than its DC counterpart—Ty navigated the vehicle onto a scenic highway. Unlike most clients who preferred the privacy and perceived status of the back seat, Lyric had chosen to sit up front beside the driver, unconsciously rejecting the hierarchical distance.

"Coming to work for the Governor?" Ty asked, his eyes remaining fixed on the road ahead.

"Not sure yet. We'll see." Lyric dodged. She was only there to explore the option of a job. Explaining all this felt like an over-share.

Lyric studied his profile, curious about the man who served as chauffeur to the politically powerful. "Do you know Governor Waylos well?"

A fleeting expression crossed Ty's face—something unreadable yet significant—before his features settled back into professional neutrality. His hands adjusted slightly on the steering wheel, his response calibrated for diplomacy.

"Yup. …Coming in and outta th'airport all the time—" Ty smoothly changed the subject, a maneuver Lyric recognized from years of interviewing reluctant sources. "Where you from?" he pivoted, "There's something in yor'talk…"

"Memphis," she replied, allowing the deflection. "This is my first time in Georgia. It's very nice."

"Thank you, kindly."

Their exchange concluded with mirrored smiles. Ty was clearly raised to well to speak ill of his employer, but his terse "yup" was all he needed to say.

Lyric turned her attention to the passing landscape—rolling hills giving way to manicured subdivisions, the carefully curated illusion of suburban southern prosperity.

***

The black SUV curved through a corridor of oak trees, their branches forming a natural canopy over the entrance to Southern Village Marketplace Mall. Sunlight filtered through the leaves, casting dappled shadows across the vehicle's hood as it approached the sprawling complex.

"Here we are. This place is all new," Ty announced, his voice carrying a hint of local pride.

The SUV slowed as they passed a gray State Police cruiser strategically positioned along the driveway. The officer inside, recognizing Ty's vehicle, offered a casual wave of acknowledgment.

"That's how you know the Governor is on the *premisees*: Her State Troopers," Ty explained, returning the officer's greeting with a respectful nod.

Lyric pressed closer to the window, taking in the manufactured charm of the upscale shopping center. Every element—from the cobblestone walkways to the wrought-iron benches—had been meticulously designed to evoke small-town nostalgia while catering to affluent tastes. The leaves on recently transplanted trees shimmered in the afternoon light, their root systems still struggling to establish themselves in foreign soil.

"They got these stores, a Brewhouse," Ty continued, gesturing toward storefronts with his right hand while maintaining perfect control of the vehicle with his left. He pointed toward an imposing brick structure with a clock tower. "And the whole second floor of this here building's your office."

The SUV pulled to a smooth stop near the lobby entrance of the main building. Through the glass doors, Lyric glimpsed a marble-floored reception area and brass-plated elevator doors.

"Elevator up in there," Ty said, shifting into park. "Good luck on the campaign, Miss Lyric."

"I—" Lyric began, intending to correct his assumption about her employment status, but something in his genuine well-wishes stopped her. "Thank you, Ty. You're very kind."

She exited the vehicle without clarifying, deciding some misconceptions weren't worth correcting. The heavy door closed behind her with a solid thunk, and she stood momentarily on the sidewalk, absorbing the surreal contrast between her regular life and this unexpected detour into political machinery.

With a deep breath, she shouldered her bag and approached the entrance. As Lyric approached the Stand Strong PAC office, a solitary yard sign in the window upstairs caught her eye. It seemed almost apologetic in its modesty, a sharp contrast to the grandiose plans she suspected were brewing behind closed doors.

The corporate suites one floor higher remained anonymous behind closed blinds, the windows betraying no signs of occupancy or activity. The brick façade gleamed in the afternoon sunlight, its newness apparent in the pristine mortar lines and unworn edges.

Lyric gripped the handle of her rolling suitcase and pushed forward toward the main lobby doors, wheels rumbling across the decorative concrete. The glass doors parted with a pneumatic hiss, welcoming her into the air-conditioned interior.

The elevator carried her upward in silence, its polished brass interior reflecting her uncertain expression. When the doors opened, Lyric stepped into a long, open office bullpen—a landscape of cubicles stretching before her like a corporate maze. Her roller bag zipped against the industrial carpet as she navigated through the mostly vacant workspace.

Empty desks dominated the floor, their barren surfaces interrupted only by occasional cardboard boxes stuffed with campaign merchandise—coffee mugs and bumper stickers emblazoned with slogans yet to find homes. The office bore the hollow atmosphere of a campaign in its embryonic stages, still awaiting the infusion of staff and energy which would transform it into a political nerv center.

In scattered cubicles throughout the space, a few lon telemarketers hunched over phones, headsets clamped to their ears as they solicited donations. The voice neares to her cooed its practiced cadence of fundraising delivery

"A donation of 3,300 is of course preferred..."

Without breaking from his script, one of the fundraisers acknowledged Lyric's presence with a flick of his thumb – back – directing her to continue toward the far end of the bullpen. She pulled her phone from her pocket, typing a quick message as she walked.

A door burst open at the end of the hallway, and David Rice emerged from his corner office, moving with the eager energy of a man desperate to impress. At thirty-five, he projected what he imagined to be political gravitas—khakis paired with dress shoes and a sport coat which strained slightly at the buttons. His receding hairline had been meticulously combed to the side, a futile attempt to disguise the inevitable advance of time.

"Lyric! Welcome! So good to see you." His voice carried across the empty space, enthusiasm bordering on desperation.

She positioned her rolling bag between them, creating a physical barrier to prevent any unwelcome embrace.

"Congrats, you wore me down." Her tone conveyed resignation rather than excitement.

"I'm so excited to have you on board—"

"No, I told you I'd take one meeting with your boss." Lyric cut him off sharply, refusing to allow him to rewrite the terms of her visit.

David's eyes tracked downward, taking in her casual denim with poorly disguised disappointment.

"You'll love her. You look good." The compliment emerged as an afterthought, a calculated addition.

Lyric's lips thinned to a narrow line at the objectification. Her gaze swept across the sparse office space.

"Only a few fundraisers?"

"Yup. Skeleton crew; contractors for now." David slipped effortlessly into campaign-speak. "'Stand Strong PAC is dedicated to common sense values of moderate—'"

"She's running." Lyric interrupted, cutting through the rehearsed pitch. "January announcement?"

A slow smile spread across David's face as he recognized her political acumen.

"You're too smart. Yeah..." His voice lowered conspiratorially. "Man! I've wanted you since day one. You could do great things here. Rada Waylos will be the frontrunner. The White House, Lyric, it's the dream."

"Your dream," she countered. "I only did one Senate race. And we lost."

"We were stuck in a comms shop led by—"

"Moving on." Her voice sliced through his excuse like a scalpel.

"It had its moments." His eyebrows lifted suggestively.

Lyric's glare could have frozen water. "No. Nothing happened between us. Just pathetic DRUNKENNESS after we lost. Where's the hire I recommended? Mira!"

She stepped away from David as a young woman emerged from a side room, large headphones dangling around her neck. Mira Gerğes, twenty-three and brimming with the unfiltered enthusiasm of youth, bounded toward Lyric. Her Lebanese American features lit up with genuine delight as she embraced her former mentor.

"Lyric! Yay!"

"Are you doing young voter work yet, like David promised, or does he have you writing his Press Advisories?" Lyric shot a pointed glare in David's direction. "Which he should be writing himself."

"Very soon, right?" Mira turned to David, seeking confirmation.

Caught in his deception, David offered an apologetic shrug before nodding affirmatively.

"I'll have a whole team! Check it—" Mira led Lyric back towards the main office rooms at the end of the bullpen, her stride eager and proud.

They passed a windowless scheduling office where several giant calendars covered the walls. An older woman wearing a telephone headset occupied the room; Mrs. Estelle Reeve, approximately sixty, paused her conversation long enough to wave at Lyric before returning to her call.

"That's Estelle, scheduling. I'm here—" Mira indicated the adjacent room, a much larger space with long bank desks and empty chairs. Her lone computer sat like an island in the sea of unclaimed workspace, its screen glowing with activity.

David hovered at their shoulders. "We really should chat before the Governor's off 'Call Time.'"

"'Beggin' for bucks.' Okay." Lyric nodded before turning to Mira. "David's lucky to have you. Lucky. Let's meet tomorrow for breakfast?"

"Dope. Thank you... for- everything..." Mira's gesture encompassed the entire office, her job –a career maybe– her gratitude evident.

"I believe in you," Lyric replied softly. "Your mom believed in me once. That's how it starts."

With a farewell wave to Mira, Lyric allowed David to guide her toward his corner office, each step taking her deeper into the political machine she'd sworn to observe rather than join.

His corner office bore all the hallmarks of a political operative with ambitions exceeding his current station— framed photos with minor political celebrities, motivational quotes positioned for visitors to notice, a desk too large for the actual work conducted upon it. Lyric perched on the edge of a chair while David claimed the couch, their positions establishing the power dynamic he desperately wanted to project.

"Think about it: a former State's Attorney, Army Reserve Officer, now she's a Governor?" David leaned forward, enthusiasm spilling from every syllable. "Plus her husband owns like six Senators. Those optics! It's like she was built in a lab!"

"I could see her as a frontrunner." Lyric's assessment came from professional observation rather than enthusiasm.

"The nominee," David corrected. "Our cash-on-hand is great. We got flush vendor accounts—"

"But!" Lyric interrupted, "Why would I leave *The Journal?*" Her question hung, direct and unadorned.

"Your oppo-research read like strategy memos. Genius stuff. We win and you're Rove to my Atwater, set for life."

Lyric's expression soured. "That's so gross. And you said Rada's a moderate, not insane. Hold that—"

Her phone buzzed with an incoming text:

Luna Cafe. 8AM?

David watched impatiently as Lyric typed her response, clearly irritated at being made to wait. She savored his discomfort, deliberately taking longer than necessary before looking up with a practiced expression of professional apology.

"Sorry. My editor. You were saying?"

"I want to hire you to be our Oppo Director. Between now and the launch. I can pay you 170 for a dossier on Rada's competitors." He shifted closer, invading her space. "Work with me. Didn't we have some fun—"

Lyric's body language closed off immediately, arms crossing as she established a clear boundary.

"No. My last night in that shitty State, I got drunk and… that kiss won't happen again. Like I said at the time."

David ignored her rejection, focusing instead on sending a text message. His dismissal of her words only fueled her anger.

"So this flirty texting of yours has to stop. I'm not interested. David."

"Okay, deal, I was playing. You gotta lighten up—and smile cuz—"

The office door swung open without warning. Governor Rada Waylos strode in with the confidence of someone accustomed to commanding rooms. At forty-nine, she exuded authority in every aspect of her appearance—her tall frame enhanced by a perfectly tailored power suit, not a hair out of place, her movements precise and deliberate.

"David! Excuse me. Hi, you're Lyric? I've heard many great things." Her handshake was firm, businesslike yet warm.

"And you recommended Mira, who is a delight. Women helping women, I love it! This is our Party too, the common-sense women of the middle. The doers."

Lyric nodded in agreement, recognizing the practiced charisma of a successful politician. Rada returned the gesture, establishing a momentary connection between them.

"David, we need to go over our endorsement rollout calendar."

"You already have a lot banked?" Lyric inquired, professional curiosity surfacing.

Rada responded with a coy shrug worthy of Shirley Temple, the practiced innocence of a politician neither confirming nor denying. Despite herself, Lyric appreciated the skillful evasion.

"Yes," David interjected. "Lyric, let's meet at 9 AM. See Estelle for your room key and stuff."

"Great meeting you, Lyric. Welcome." Rada's farewell carried the certainty of someone who'd closed a deal, though Lyric had committed to nothing.

She bit her tongue rather than correct the assumption as David escorted her from his office. Lyric watched as he and the Governor disappeared into Rada's much larger office suite at the end of the hallway. Despite her reservations about David, she couldn't deny being impressed by Governor Waylos—the woman possessed the magnetic quality essential to successful politicians.

Wandering back through the bullpen, Lyric's attention snagged on a figure stretching languidly in an office chair. The man's physical beauty registered like a physical impact—Cal Druck, thirty-three, possessed the kind of effortless good looks advertising agencies tried and failed to manufacture. His hair fell in perfect waves, his body radiating fitness without the straining desperation of a gym addict. A genuine smile bloomed across Lyric's face before she could suppress it.

"Hey. Who are you?"

"Lyric. Who are you?" She matched his direct approach.

"Cal. Lyric-Cal. If we became a couple, that'd be absurd." His observation carried playful confidence rather than presumption.

"Luckily you look more like a Calvin." She parried smoothly.

"I'm open to change—so our first date can be tonight then. Yes? Lyric?" His performance of debonair charm held enough self-awareness to avoid arrogance, eliciting another smile from Lyric.

"Sure. Where were you—before?"

"With the Governor. Sometimes while—"

"Call-Time babysitter, oh I remember." She completed his thought, demonstrating her familiarity with campaign operations.

"We all have to debase ourselves, don't we, in their lofty service?"

Lyric chuckled, appreciating his irreverence. "OK. What do you do, really though?"

"Little a'this little a'that. Whatever the boss needs—I aim to please." His gaze intensified, charged with unmistakable sexual energy.

"What do you do? Lyric."

"Same. Lately I eat shit." Her blunt assessment cut through pretense.

"Yep. Did they give you a townhouse? Or are you here, up in the suites?" He gestured upward, indicating the floors above them.

"I dunno. Gotta talk to...Estelle?"

"Well, I'm in Room 13, upstairs." Cal extended his phone toward her, an invitation rather than a demand.

Lyric accepted, typing her number into his contacts. The casual exchange carried none of the discomfort she'd experienced with David's attention.

"So I'll call you later? Show you the 'Southern Village Marketplace' life."

She pressed the call button before returning his phone, ensuring her own device would capture his number. On cue, her handbag buzzed with the incoming call.

"Then I'll see you soon...Calvin." She allowed a hint of playfulness to color her voice.

Cal smiled as he ended the call, leaning in close enough for Lyric to catch the faint scent of mint on his breath.

"It's Caleb. Shhh..." The mock-secret was shared as a conspiracy between equals.

Lyric returned his playfulness with a wink before turning toward Estelle's scheduling office. Only when her back was safely turned did she allow her face to betray her astonishment—the surprised delight of unexpected chemistry in the most unlikely of locations.

****

The corridor of the corporate housing wing stretched before Lyric, a neutral beige hallway punctuated by identical doors with brass numbers. She paused outside Room 13, knuckles rapping against the polished wood. The hollow echo of her knock reverberated through the empty hallway. No answer.

Brow furrowing, she retrieved her phone and typed a quick message to Cal. Seconds stretched into a minute. Her weight shifted from one foot to the other, annoyance beginning to surface when a ping announced an incoming text:

15.

The correction was so brief it nearly qualified as cryptic. Lyric pivoted, scanning the numbers on the doors until she located Room 15 at the far end of the hallway back near the elevator. She approached with renewed purpose, rapping sharply on the door.

It swung open almost immediately to reveal Cal, his magnificent form draped only in a white towel slung precariously around his hips. Water droplets clung to his skin, catching the light as they traced paths down his chest. His hair, darkened by moisture, curled against his forehead in a way professional stylists spent hours trying to recreate.

"You said—" Lyric began, her prepared admonishment dying on her lips.

"This bathroom's bigger. Come in." Cal stepped aside, the invitation casual and confident.

Momentarily stunned by the tableau before her, Lyric hesitated at the threshold. Her hesitation lasted only seconds before curiosity and attraction propelled her forward into the master suite.

The room opened before her—spacious and luxurious by campaign housing standards. A king-sized bed dominated the space, crisp white linens contrasting with the rich walnut of the headboard. Floor-to-ceiling windows offered views of the marketplace below, now bathed in late afternoon light.

Lyric's attention, however, remained fixed on Cal as he moved through the space. His broad shoulders tapered to a narrow waist, muscles shifting beneath smooth skin with each motion. The towel barely concealed the perfect curve of his buttocks. She found herself following his movement with unconscious appreciation.

"Gol-ly, this wasn't the plan..." Cal turned, leaning against the wall opposite the bed, his posture relaxed yet somehow deliberately inviting. His eyes held hers with unwavering intensity.

She stood frozen, unaware her lips had parted slightly. The air between them crackled with unspoken possibility. Lyric realized she'd been holding her breath only when she needed to speak.

"I needed a shower too—" The words emerged more breathless than she'd intended.

"Great—" Cal's response came instantly.

"But I forgot shampoo..." Lyric paused, maintaining the pretense of practicality. "Are you done?"

"...Not yet..." His voice dropped lower, the suggestion unmistakable. "Wanna share?"

The proposition hung between them, straightforward yet laden with promise. No games, no pretense—an honest invitation. Light spilled from the open bathroom door, warm and inviting. Steam still curled from within, evidence of the shower recently abandoned.

"Yeah." Lyric swallowed, decision crystallizing. "Yeah I do. Let's go."

With newfound boldness, she reached forward and tugged at his towel. It surrendered easily, pooling at his feet. Cal smiled, utterly at ease in his nakedness, a man comfortable in his physical glory.

Lyric stepped out of her shoes, the first small concession to what would follow. Cal extended his hand, fingers intertwining with hers as he guided her toward the bathroom, their skin contrasting—his still damp from the shower, hers warm and dry.

The transition from bedroom to bathroom took mere seconds, yet shifted everything between them. The instant the door closed behind them, restraint evaporated. Their bodies collided against the tiled wall, lips meeting with hungry urgency. Cal's hands slid beneath her sweater, pushing the fabric upward, while Lyric fumbled with the top button of her jeans, fingers clumsy with desire.

Cal dropped to one knee, assuming a position of supplication as he pulled at her denim. The sight of him kneeling before her sent a wave of pleasure through Lyric's body. A moan escaped her lips as she tilted her head backward, surrendering to sensation.

Reaching blindly for the shower controls, she twisted the knob. Water cascaded from above, resuming its rhythmic drumming against the tile.

"Get in here." The command came as a breathless invitation as she pulled Cal to his feet.

Together they stepped into the generous shower stall, warm water enveloping them both. It sluiced between their bodies as they pressed together, hands exploring newly revealed terrain. Their kisses deepened, grew more urgent. Cal lifted her slightly, strong arms supporting her weight as she wrapped herself around him.

The world beyond the steam-filled bathroom ceased to exist. There was only sensation—water streaming over heated skin, the press of lips, the exploration of hands, the melding of bodies in ancient rhythm.

***

Dusk painted the sky in watercolor hues of lavender and amber, the fading light filtering through the half-drawn blinds. In the king-sized bed, tangled in sheets still damp from their bodies, Lyric and Cal lay in satiated contentment. Cal's eyes were closed, his breathing slowed to the rhythm of near-sleep. His hand traced lazy patterns across Lyric's skin, fingertips whispering over the curve of her hip.

"I could tell right away you're not like them. You're real." His voice carried the drowsy intimacy of post-coital bliss.

Lyric's eyes remained open, her mind already racing ahead while her body lingered in present pleasure. The intimate setting had heightened her observational skills rather than dulling them. Details she'd missed upon first entering the room now demanded acknowledgment.

"OK, let's be real: There's makeup in the bathroom, women's shoes in the closet." Her tone shifted toward journalistic inquiry. "'Social Media Consultant???'"

Cal's hand stilled on her skin. "Hey, I have a camera. What do you do?"

"This is the Governor's suite." The statement hung between them, neither accusation nor question—merely established fact.

"She...rarely stays here." His hesitation conveyed volumes.

"But whenever she does—" Lyric pressed.

"Seriously, what do you do?" Cal redirected, professional deflection masked as casual curiosity.

"I'm an investigator." Lyric allowed the redirect temporarily. "But whenever—"

"That tracks. Like, you're a cop?"

"No, I debunk lies." When confusion crossed his features, she clarified: "...I work in journalism."

"Cool! That's—that's very honorable." His enthusiasm seemed genuine, if somewhat surprised.

"Well, I'm a fact-checker." Vulnerability crept into her admission. "Would I like to contribute to a story? I mean, who wouldn't love a byline, right? Even once."

Cal shifted to see her more fully, responding to the rare glimpse beneath her armor. She continued, voice softening with the admission of ambition.

"To be able to say I did it. ...'In service of truth.'"

"Wow. You will." His encouragement was immediate, devoid of condescension. "I'd love to read yo—"

Lyric pivoted again, returning to her earlier line of questioning. "So what's the truth? Hm? Do you 'aim to please' the Governor whenever she wants?"

"Are you mad I'm not a virgin?" His question carried teasing humor rather than defensiveness.

She laughed, the tension dissolving. "No. But I am...hungry."

"Great. Me too."

Cal's lips found hers again before trailing downward, across her collarbone, between her breasts, across her abdomen. Each kiss elicited another laugh from Lyric, pleasure rippling through her as tension melted away. Her laughter—open, unguarded—filled the room as the last light of day faded from the sky, leaving them enveloped in the intimate darkness of evening.

SATURDAY

The buzzing of Lyric's phone cut through the peaceful morning quiet, the screen illuminating with "CALL FROM MIRA" as it vibrated against the wooden top of the bedside table.

Lyric stirred awake, her naked body draped across Cal's equally bare form. The morning light filtered through half-drawn blinds, casting slanted rays across their entwined limbs. Despite her exhaustion, a smile played on her lips—the kind born from profound contentment rather than mere happiness. She stretched toward her insistent phone, muscles aching in the most satisfying way. An empty pizza box lay open on the floor, a testament to their need for sustenance during twelve hours of passionate connection.

Reality intruded as she remembered her scheduled breakfast meeting. The realization struck her—she was late.

"Mira. Sorry. Slept through my alarm—" Lyric mumbled into the phone, voice still thick with sleep.

Behind her, Cal awakened. His strong hands found her waist, fingers pressing into her skin with gentle insistence, silently pleading for her to remain. He maneuvered himself up behind her, propping himself on one elbow, his body curved against hers in a perfect parenthesis.

"I'm almost ready. Ten minutes," Lyric promised into the phone, trying to sound more put-together than she was.

"Me too," Cal whispered, his breath warm against her ear.

Lyric turned sharply, pressing a finger to her lips to silence him. Her gaze traveled downward over his form, her eyes widening with unmistakable appreciation for what she discovered below.

"Fifteen minutes. Okay, bye—" she amended hastily, hanging up as Cal's mouth found her neck.

The phone slipped from her fingers, landing with a soft thud on the carpet below as she surrendered to his touch.

"My God, you ARE ready," her voice floated from beyond the edge of the bed, words dissolving into a sigh.

***

The morning dew dampened Lyric's sneakers as she sprinted across the Southern Village Green. The quaint shops around the perimeter stood in stark contrast to her chaotic energy. She ran with purpose toward Luna Cafe, its blue awning like a beacon in the morning sunlight.

Lyric burst through the door of Luna Cafe, her face flushed from exertion. The aroma of freshly ground coffee beans and baked goods wrapped around her as she wove between tables toward her waiting friend. Mira sat primly at a corner table, a study in contrasts to Lyric's disheveled state.

"Sorry!" Lyric exclaimed, dropping into the chair across from Mira, whose expression conveyed both amusement and mild disapproval.

Mira's eyes raked over Lyric's attire—the same worn jeans from yesterday. "The jeans—again? It tends to be a bit more conservative here."

Her scrutiny continued upward, noting the familiar sweater. A tiny crease formed between her brows.

Lyric shifted in her seat, attempting to reclaim her usual role as the wise mentor. "Right. How are you? How's this campaign compare to the last?"

Her attempt at professional conversation crumbled as her gaze landed on Mira's paper coffee cup. The barista had scrawled "Meow" across the white surface instead of "Mira." Laughter bubbled up from her chest, uncontained.

"Mira to Meow?! How's that happen?" she asked, pointing at the cup.

Mira's mouth tightened. "Same way Randhawa Raj-Kaur becomes Rada. 'Racism.'"

The word hung heavy between them. Lyric's smile faded. "Impossible. So. What's your gut sense of the Governor?"

"Frontrunner, easy. But. I mean..." Mira glanced at her watch, rising from her seat. "It's a long question and I have to be at the office before everybody else."

As Mira prepared to leave, Lyric reached out, her finger catching Mira's sleeve. Something akin to worry clouded her expression.

"Are you a true believer?" The question carried more weight than its words suggested.

"No. I'm always early. David brags about staying late early's my thing."

Concern deepened the lines around Lyric's eyes. "Are you two...close?"

"Hell no." Mira's response came swift and definitive. "Are you...?"

A sharp whistle interrupted their exchange. Both women turned toward the sound.

Cal stood in line at the counter, gesturing toward Lyric with a questioning expression, silently asking if she wanted anything. She dismissed him with a wave—pleasant but resolute.

When Lyric returned her attention to Mira, she noticed the cold appraisal in her friend's eyes as they tracked Cal—the slight tightening of her jaw suggesting more than casual dislike.

"No. Good." Lyric's voice dropped lower. "Can we talk at lunch?"

"Yeah, come grab me. See ya." Mira departed with another backward glance at Cal, who approached Lyric's table.

"You didn't get anything?" he asked, slipping into the chair Mira had vacated.

In one fluid motion, Lyric snagged the plastic bottle from his hand and unscrewed the cap. "I got this purple smoothie." She took a long sip before he could protest.

Cal reached for Mira's abandoned cup, turning it to read the name. "Meow. Who the hell is Meow?"

"Me. Cat Power. Call me Chan," Lyric replied, the corners of her mouth curving upward as confusion spread across his handsome face.

"Never heard of Cat Power? She's a musician. She also goes by 'Chan,'" she explained, watching his bewilderment grow.

"If your name is Cat Power, why would you go by Chan?!" The perplexity in his voice was genuine.

"Well, Caleb, people change their names all the time if it's worth it." Her eyes locked with his, conveying more than her casual tone suggested.

"True. It really was," he admitted, a private understanding passing between them.

"You too," she affirmed softly.

Cal shrugged with charming nonchalance. "You're friends with Mira? That girl—"

"Is not a fan of you, huh?" Lyric finished, head tilted in observation.

His shrug communicated a carefree "Can't win 'em all" attitude, but the arrival of a waitress interrupted their exchange.

Eager to please, the woman placed a bagel on a small plate before Cal, her movements deliberate, her smile too bright. "Toasted, just how you like it."

"Trish. You really didn't have to..." Cal replied, discomfort evident in his voice despite his polite smile.

Lyric's gaze swept across the cafe, noticing for the first time what she'd missed upon entry. Several young mothers in yoga attire watched Cal with undisguised interest, their conversations paused mid-sentence, attention fixed on him like compass needles to north.

"Let's go for a walk, whaddya say?" Lyric proposed, rising from her chair.

They left the waitress standing by their table, disappointment etched on her features. As they navigated toward the exit, Lyric glanced back at the yoga-clad mothers. Their eyes followed Cal—and by extension, her—with thinly veiled envy.

The weight of their collective stare pressed against her back as she pushed through the door into the morning air.

***

Morning sunlight warmed the grassy oval of the Southern Village Green as Lyric and Cal shared his bagel on a wooden bench. Sparrows hopped near their feet, darting forward whenever a crumb fell. Their eyes met between bites, exchanging silent amusements—the kind of wordless communication reserved for new lovers still discovering each other's quirks.

"Well, yes. I do," Cal admitted, tearing off another piece of bagel. "I do know some of those women. But-"

"Unreal." Lyric shook her head, a half-smile playing on her lips.

"Why!? I teach Acro-Pilates at the Body Therapy studio. Right there." He gestured across the Green toward a sleek storefront with minimalist signage and floor-to-ceiling windows. Inside, shadows moved through morning routines. They're his students, Lyric realized.

Lyric laughed, the sound genuine and unrestrained. "Acro-Pilates!? What!? What a life."

Her laughter contained no malice, only wonder at the contrast between their worlds—hers filled with pressure and his with... whatever Acro-Pilates entailed.

"I prefer you," Cal said, his eyes steady on hers.

"The Governor doesn't get you off?" Lyric asked, one eyebrow arched.

Cal's expression hardened, surprising her with its sudden intensity. "She thinks she's God's gift. Rich people, man; selfish toxic privilege."

"Yikes. Tell me how you really feel." Lyric studied his face, searching for the source of his vehemence.

"I told you four times."

"Fair." She paused, choosing her next words carefully. "What are you gonna do when this...ruse is up?"

His response came with casual nonchalance. "Maybe I'll write a book about Rada."

Lyric stiffened, bagel forgotten in her hand. "Whoa. You're kidding, right???"

Cal smiled dismissively, but something flickered behind his eyes—a calculation, a consideration. It unsettled her.

"Everyone's careers—" she began, voice tight.

"I was kidding!" he interrupted, hands raised in mock surrender.

Lyric narrowed her eyes, examining him as she might examine political opposition research. His inability to maintain eye contact spoke volumes. Cal possessed many talents, but lying to Lyric clearly wasn't among them.

"I have to teach a class—can we talk about this later? Lunch?" he asked, already gathering himself to leave.

"I have a date. And a meeting soon." Lyric felt professional distance reasserting itself. Would he let it stay?

Cal leaned closer, the scent of him—clean sweat and bagel—filling her nostrils. "Lyric...when can I see you next? Hey… I like you. I'm serious."

"I'll find you." Her voice soft, happy that he seemed to be for real.

He kissed her—quick, impulsive—and he sprinted across the Green toward his studio. Lyric watched him go, smiling because she recognized sincerity when she heard it, even if it complicated matters she preferred to keep simple.

The thought crossed Lyric's mind: was Cal enough of a reason to take this job if there were David-sized drawbacks?

***

The morning light slanted through the windows of Rada's expansive office suite. The room smelled of expensive perfume, furniture polish, and ambition. Lyric sat with perfect posture in a leather visitor's chair, dressed in fresh clothing—a navy blazer over a crisp white blouse paired with charcoal slacks. Every element of her appearance now projected professionalism and competence as she took notes on a legal pad, her handwriting precise and measured.

Rada stood behind an imposing desk, her tailored silk suit emphasizing her slender frame. David occupied a chair beside the desk, his body language deferential yet somehow presumptuous. The power dynamic crystallized before Lyric's eyes—Rada as the unquestioned authority, David as the eager lieutenant, herself as... what? The hired gun? The mercenary talent?

Rada tapped a document on her desk with one bony finger. Her massive diamond wedding band caught the light, sending tiny rainbows dancing across the paper. "These rivals must be stopped. Now. Scare them out of the race before they start. We need more leaks—"

"Uh, media strategy is outside the scope of Lyric's oppo work," David interjected, his voice smooth yet condescending.

Lyric straightened, her pen hovering above paper. This was the first overt attempt to diminish her capabilities, and she refused to let it pass unchallenged.

"I AM a strategist, David." Her tone brooked no argument.

Rada nodded, her dark eyes calculating. "And you hav
great press connections. Rumors will blaze if someon
trusted like you confirms the validity."

"Cue up the, uh, '*New Scrutiny Over...*' headlines. Those hi
hard." David smirked, leaning back in his chair.

"Senator Nordström's charitable arm being a fraud is :
perfect example," Rada continued, moving toward the
window with regal grace.

"But one's actually a lie. I—" Lyric began, alarm bell:
ringing in her mind.

"Too late." Rada cut her off with a dismissive wave. "'A
lie travels twice around the world while the truth is still
putting on its shoes.'" She wiggled her head in a self-
satisfied gesture, reminiscent of a subtle south-Asian
touchdown celebration.

David leaned forward, his eyes gleaming. "If you can,
we'd prefer scandals about extra-marital affairs. Stupid-
ass media people eat crap up."

Lyric rotated slightly in her chair, angling her body away
from David. The casual way he spoke about sex repulsed
her, as if he were discussing menu options rather than
potentially destroying lives.

"Actually, my husband's firm might have use for your
work too—" Rada mused, examining her manicure.
"Either way, I like tying my opposition to climate change
radicals."

A line existed somewhere in the murky waters of political
strategy—a boundary between aggressive campaigning
and outright dishonesty. Lyric sensed she had found it.

"I can't manufacture connections," she said, her voice quiet but firm.

David snorted. "No. Plant rumors. Our people will print those '*Sources suggest…*' hits. Then we hire a troll farm to hype it online. Who's gonna be trusted? An Army Officer, billionaire Governor—or a nobody? You know who."

The practiced ease with which they discussed manipulation chilled her. These were not people who happened to cross ethical lines in moments of weakness—they bulldozed through boundaries with premeditation.

"That's—" Lyric began, disgust rising like bile in her throat. Yet her face remained pleasant, her smile fixed in place. This job—which had seemed so promising—now revealed itself as something else entirely. But this was not the moment for confrontation. The weekend stretched before them, and bridges could be burned on Monday.

"—true. Let me look into this. Great." Lyric accepted the paper with Rada's rivals' names, her fingers careful not to touch Rada's.

For a fraction of a second, her mask slipped. Neither Rada nor David noticed—too engrossed in their own machinations—but Lyric knew with crystalline clarity she would never work for these people. Some prices were too high, even for career advancement.

***

Outside the Body Therapy Studio, sunlight bounced off the polished storefront glass as Lyric stood watching Cal lead his class. Her lips curved into a bemused smile. Inside, ten women clad in expensive Lululemon attire contorted into impossible positions, their eyes never straying far from their instructor. Cal moved among them with practiced grace, his T-shirt darkened with sweat in appealing patterns across his broad shoulders. The class wound down, participants exhaling final breaths as he brought them back to reality.

The studio air hung heavy with exertion when Lyric pushed through the glass door. The scent of eucalyptus oil from diffusers mingled with sweat, creating an oddly intimate atmosphere. A few students lingered, stretching on mats or gathering belongings from cubbies along the wall. Several clustered around Cal, laughing too enthusiastically at something he said.

His eyes lit up when he spotted Lyric. He extracted himself from a conversation with a blonde woman whose disappointment was palpable when he walked away mid-sentence.

"You found me," he said, grinning that Lyric made good on her promise to see him again. He turned toward the dispersing class. "Good work! Ladies. See ya soon. Bye."

As Cal's students filed past Lyric toward the exit, each woman assessed her with sidelong glances. Some narrowed their eyes; others lifted their chins in subtle challenge. The primal display of jealousy might have amused Lyric under different circumstances.

"I need to talk to you," she said, keeping her voice low.

Cal nodded, reading her serious expression. "This way. Don't want you caught in this schmoozing...part of the job." He rolled his eyes, acknowledging the performance aspect of his role.

She followed him down a narrow hallway where the bright, airy aesthetic of the main studio gave way to utility—exposed pipes, bare concrete, emergency exit signs casting red shadows. The temperature dropped several degrees away from the heated studio space.

They pushed through a metal door into the harsh midday sun. Behind the main building stretched a utilitarian area—dumpsters lined against the cement wall of the building's rear, sporadic parking spaces, delivery access points. The crafted facade of the brick and grass village green seemed miles away rather than yards.

Lyric began her prepared speech: "Your 'department' bought camera gear, but you've posted no video. You make eight grand a month. I'm worried," Lyric said, her voice edged with concern.

She handed him a printed sheet—numbers, dates, expenditures circled in red. His eyes scanned it, expression unchanging.

"I got this from 5 minutes of digging. You're *too* obviously...a kept pet. You have to protect yourself."

The words hung between them. No sugar-coating, no easing into it.

"I got it under control," Cal replied, his shoulders tensing.

"Because you have insurance? Is it a sex video? Because then your scam is too obvious. I'm really—"

"Heyyyyy…" Cal halted, glancing around the parking lot. Her volume had risen with her concern. He tilted his head, indicating they should continue walking but speak more quietly.

They continued up the back parking lot's sidewalk toward to the main entrance's back door. The lobby gleamed with polished marble floors and steel fixtures. Cal pressed the elevator button, his eyes drifting up to a security camera mounted in the corner. The camera's red light blinked steadily, recording their every move. Lyric held her tongue as Cal seemed to wish.

The elevator arrived with a soft ding. They stepped inside, both silent until the doors closed.

Inside, she began to speak but Cal motioned to continue holding.

Cal's real room, number 13, sat near the start of a carpeted hallway of additional bedroom suites. He unlocked it with a keycard, and they entered quickly.

The space bore little evidence of habitation—generic hotel-like furnishings, minimal personal items. A bed dominated the small room, impeccably made. The closet door stood ajar, revealing a sparse selection of clothing.

Cal closed his door with a definitive click and then began in earnest:

"I'm not running a scam. I'm—" He paused, choosing his words. "She made it clear I'd be in trouble if I left."

Lyric's expression shifted from concern to alarm. "Are…are you being blackmailed?"

He hesitated, weighing his response. The situation defied simple categorization, and his face reflected internal conflict.

"I'm paid well," was his first shrugging thought. "I dunno, maybe this's all I can do; be a toy for-"

"No!" Lyric cut him off. "This is generally something women deal with; So I get it. Look, you said you'd write a book about Rada—"

"I said I was kidding." His voice hardened.

"—what if there's another way?"

Cal studied her face, searching for judgment. "What do you mean? …You're not mad?"

"Not at you. This place sucks. Those two bring out the worst in each other."

Understanding dawned in his eyes—her anger targeted Rada and David, not him. His expression softened with relief.

She really was different than the others.

"You can take it out on me," he suggested, a small smile playing at the corner of his mouth. The implication was unmistakable.

"Work up a sweat on you? You mean?" Lyric asked, one eyebrow raised. When he nodded, she added in a blurt, "Gotta be quick—"

With a primal sound caught between a laugh and a growl, she launched herself at him. He caught her easily, his strong arms wrapping around her thighs as she straddled him. They tumbled onto the bed in a tangle of limbs and laughter. Cal yanked off his sweatshirt in one fluid motion, flinging it toward the window. The fabric struck the vertical blinds, sending slivers of sunlight dancing.

***

Sunlight found David's eye as he peeked out his office window blinds while waiting on hold on a phone call when Lyric entered with a cough, no knock.

She stood ramrod straight back by his door. Her professional demeanor had returned fully—hair smoothed, clothes pristine, expression neutral. David acknowledged her with a nod but continued his conversation.

He gestured toward a leather couch against the wall. She remained standing – her eyes moved around David's lair.

David's office exuded authority through calculated austerity—no family photos, minimal art, expensive furnishings chosen for status rather than comfort. He stood by the window, adjusting vertical blinds as he muttered into his phone. Sunlight filtered through dingy glass.

Finally, he ended his call with exaggerated importance. "Great. I booked a staff retreat to one of the Governor's vacation homes. Hilton Head. Ever been?"

"One of. No." Lyric paused, gathering herself. "I appreciate this invite, but I can't accept your job offer."

David's smile never faltered. "The Governor expected this. She said 'no way would you take anything less than Director-level Strategist.'"

The unexpected promotion caught Lyric off-guard. In other circumstances, this opportunity would have been a dream.

"If you're our Key Strategist, you could leave here and start your own strategy shop!" David continued, watching her reaction. "The Governor said she'd set you up with all the Campaign Committees. More clients than you could ever handle. Her husband, Randall Waylos—billionaire, will invest. You'll make millions."

His casual mention of others' wealth and influence revealed a man comfortable playing with other people's power. He relished his proximity to power. The glossy promises rolled off his tongue with practiced ease.

"I know—amazing. So before you decide anything, PLEASE sleep on it? Then, if you want to take the jet back, it's fine. Hell, fly anywhere."

The blatant corruption stunned her. Lyric lowered herself onto the couch, recalling another piece of the puzzle. Lyric's tone shifted to goad David into assuming her answer will soon be "yes."

Lyric pretended to remember suddenly, "Oh, Rada said something about me also working for her husband. What's this?"

David's smile widened. "Randall. I could tell you about it in the pool on Hilton Head Island?"

"How about you tell me now." Her tone left no room for deflection.

"There's some double-dipping with Randall's hedge fund," David shrugged, cavalier about potential felonies. "Like, right now he's helping Russians buy oil fields in Alaska. We help twist some arms."

The criminal implications solidified her decision. Lyric stood, now certain of her answer. She forced herself to continue smiling through the disgust.

"Wow—I will sleep on it, David." Her voice revealed nothing of her internal certainty to flee.

"I figured you'd stick around a few days, so I put you on our per-diem." He handed her a cash envelope with "Lyric" scrawled across it in blue ink.

She accepted it with a polite nod, turned on her heel, and strode out into the bullpen.

She spotted Mira through the open door of her office and leaned in.

"Lunch!" she called, injecting warmth into her voice for the first time since leaving Cal.

Mira's head snapped up from her computer screen, her face brightening. She leaped from her chair, eager to escape with her friend and mentor. Whatever Lyric's complicated feelings about this place, her connection with Mira remained uncomplicated—a spark of authenticity amid the corruption.

***

Doctor Burger buzzed with the energy of a trendy bistro at peak hours—exposed brick walls, vintage light fixtures dangling from high ceilings, and bartenders crafting artisanal sodas behind a reclaimed wood counter. Through the floor-to-ceiling windows, patrons could observe the Southern Village Green, where dog-walkers and lunch-breakers traversed the manicured lawn.

Lyric sat across from Mira in a corner booth, her untouched burger growing cold on its wooden serving board. The restaurant's ambient chatter provided a soundtrack to her brooding thoughts, each laugh or clink of glasses a jarring counterpoint to her darkening mood. Her mind replayed the morning's conversations with David and Rada on endless loop.

"What's wrong?" Mira asked, wiping ketchup from the corner of her mouth.

Lyric's gaze focused somewhere beyond the window. "Some people...should never get power."

"David," Mira said, not a question but a confirmation of shared understanding.

"Both," Lyric's eyes came back to Mira. "I thought she was a moderate, but they're wingnuts. And reckless—this campaign is a time-bomb."

Lyric lowered her voice, leaning across the reclaimed wood table. "We should not stay here. I'm leaving, but I haven't told anybody yet so..."

Mira's eyes widened. "Secret." Mira paused, processing. "Are you saying I should quit?"

Lyric nodded, her expression somber. "I can try to get you a job in D.C."

"Is that a promise?" Mira asked, hope and wariness mingling in her voice.

"You were a great intern. ...Your mom helped me land my job." Guilt crept into Lyric's tone. "I'm so sorry your first experience..."

Mira smiled, a genuine expression breaking through her professional mask. Mira touched Lyric's hand. All was forgiven.

Lyric lifted her fountain drink, offering a toast, "To Dr. Leyla Gerğes."

"To mom, and her favorite student."

Their paper cups met with a soft tap before they both sipped through striped straws. The moment of connection eased some of the tension from Lyric's shoulders.

"Can you tell me what's so reckless?" Mira asked, dropping her voice to match Lyric's conspiratorial tone.

"Nope." Lyric finally bit into her burger, signaling an end to serious conversation.

***

The autumn afternoon sun cast long shadows across the Village Green as Lyric stood beneath the gazebo. Its white-painted wooden lattice created dappled patterns on her skin. She stared up at the luxury condo suites rising beyond the trees, pocketing her phone as a familiar figure emerged from the elevator lobby across the street.

Cal jogged toward her, weaving between pedestrians. His face brightened upon seeing her, one hand raised to display his phone—evidence he'd received her message. He moved with the unconscious grace of someone perpetually in motion, crossing the grass with effortless strides.

He dropped beside her on the gazebo bench, pressing a quick kiss to her cheek before she halted him with an upraised palm.

"…Would you be okay…if there's no big payday for you? Your book idea," she asked, studying his reaction.

"For safety. Fucking laws don't apply to billionaires. It's scary—" His easy demeanor cracked, revealing genuine apprehension beneath.

"Today they asked me to break, like, a buncha laws, no biggie—so you're—"

"Right. So if a book makes me famous, she can't touch me. How's all." His logic, while twisted, followed its own coherent path.

Lyric nodded, processing his reasoning. "So what if you can get safe—quietly? Come to DC and play the sex tape for my paper. You can keep the file."

Panic flashed across Cal's face. "What would do? Fuu…I revealed there is a video. Didn't I?"

Disappointment in himself mingled with embarrassment. Lyric's expression softened with guilt—she'd extracted the confirmation through interrogation tactics worthy of her profession.

"Okay, so what?" Cal asked, regrouping.

"*The Journal* will probably cut a deal with her. She'd quietly drop out, no story. They'd help save the Party."

"And me? What do I do?" Uncertainty tinged his question.

"You…could stay in DC? With me??" The invitation emerged more tentatively than she'd intended.

He searched her face for signs of insincerity, finding none. A smile spread across his features as he absorbed her offer—and what lay behind it.

"Dag. I get paid on the first of the month...Can I move in November 2nd???"

"Ohmygod, you're a ridiculous person." His exasperation lacked any real frustration.

"But we're a lotta fun. Let's do this!" Cal kissed her cheek quickly.

Lyric responded by pulling him into a deeper kiss. When they parted, she murmured, "...Yeah. But I leave tomorrow—"

"You're mine tonight." He captured her hand in his, their fingers interlacing.

A flush rose to her cheeks—partly from desire, partly from triumph. The complex game she'd entered unknowingly had somehow transformed into something here that she actually wanted to win.

***

The evening unfolded in a series of vignettes, each moment etching itself into Lyric's memory:

Mary Belle's Gifts smelled of potpourri and scented candles, shelves crowded with tacky souvenirs and local crafts. Lyric and Cal ambled through narrow aisles, their shoulders brushing against each other. He carried her jacket draped over one arm, a gentlemanly gesture she found adorable.

"To remember this weekend," Cal said, holding up a garish magnet shaped like Georgia, complete with a cartoon peach and glitter-infused resin.

"And you are?" Lyric arched an eyebrow.

He clutched his chest in mock heartbreak, his theatrical response drawing a smile from Lyric despite herself.

Outside Bingo's Bookstore, Cal paused before the entrance, studying a sign posted on the glass door. Lyric strode inside, breathing in the comforting scent of paper and uncracked binding glue. When she turned to share an observation with Cal, her jaw dropped.

He sauntered in, bare-chested, his discarded shirt tucked into his back pocket.

"What's 'no shirt no service' mean?" he asked, feigning innocence while other patrons stared.

"It means I won't service you." Lyric pushed him toward the exit, shooting apologetic glances at the tall clerk whose expression wavered between amusement and annoyance.

In Always 21 Boutique, pop music thumped through overhead speakers while mannequins posed in impossible configurations. Lyric stood at the counter, counting bills from her wallet for a gray canvas tote bag emblazoned with the feminist slogan "Nevertheless, She Persisted" in bold typography.

Movement from the changing area caught her attention. Cal emerged wearing a tiny pink pleather vest stretched across his chest and a miniature hat perched at a jaunty angle on his head. Both items were clearly designed for someone a quarter of his size.

"What if you introduce me to your parents like this?" he asked, striking a model's pose.

Without missing a beat, Lyric handed cash to the funky cashier with bright blue hair. "He's not affiliated with me."

The Blue Ridge Distillery and Brewhouse cultivated rustic chic with its copper fixtures and barrel tables. Dim lighting cast amber shadows across their booth as a glum waiter refilled water glasses – eyeing the two annoyed that they were happy drunks but he was working.

Lyric and Cal attacked plates of golden fried chicken, grease shining on their fingers and lips. A flight of whiskey samples sat between them, several glasses already emptied. The alcohol had loosened their tongues and lowered inhibitions.

"—but even more generally, without blackmail, there's like a certain amount of sexual objectification we're supposed to put up with," Lyric said, her words slightly slurred but her mind sharp.

"Preach. I feel you, man." Cal raised a glass in solidarity.

"I mean, does she even take you to her vacation homes?"

"No way. I'm work pet." His casual acceptance of his position both disturbed and intrigued her.

"How many does she have?" Lyric asked, professional curiosity surfacing through her inebriation.

"Hilton Head, Antigua, Bermuda—" Cal paused, eyeing her. "Or do you mean pets? Are you investigating?"

"I'm venting. I'll stop." She lifted another whiskey sample. "But I will not stop drinking this. What's this!?"

Cal consulted the menu, squinting at small print. "Defiant." He grinned. "Want a bottle? My treat."

"Thank you," Lyric said, genuine appreciation in her voice. "What do you want?"

"To take off my shirt, get kicked out." His delivery remained deadpan.

"May I suggest an alternate venue?" Her eyes danced with promise.

Cal downed his remaining shot in one swift motion, slamming the empty glass onto the table with a sharp crack. "Yes!"

The world spun as they stumbled into Rada's master suite, a tangle of limbs and discarded clothing. Lyric and Cal stumbled through the door of Rada's master suite, a tangle of limbs, lips locked, hands fumbling with each other's clothes.

Their giggles bounced around the room as Lyric shrugged off her green jacket, draping it haphazardly over a nearby chair.

Cal kicked free of his pants with boyish eagerness while Lyric wiggled out of her dress in exaggerated, playful movements. She leapt onto the king-sized bed with abandon, her body sinking into the plush mattress. The lamplight caressed the curves of her silhouette.

Cal stood frozen at the foot of the bed, his naked form statuesque in the half-light. Lyric's underwear sailed through the air, hitting him squarely in the face—yet he remained immobile, eyes fixed on his phone screen. The blue light illuminated the sudden concern growing across his features.

"Uh-oh..." Cal's voice cracked the silence. "Randall went to Turkey for business. Rada's coming here."

Time seemed to crystallize around them. The mention of Governor Rada's husband served as a stark reminder of the precarious nature of their liaison.

"Tonight?" Lyric's voice held none of the laughter from seconds before.

"Right now. ...You have to go—" Cal scrambled across the room, retrieving Lyric's scattered belongings—her underwear, shoes, various items transformed from romantic accessories to evidence.

Lyric struggled to dress, her movements clumsy and panicked. The alcohol in her system turned simple tasks into complex challenges. Their previous laughter now replaced by urgent, hushed commands.

"She's in the elevator!" Cal breathed, his voice pitched with panic. "There's emergency stairs—hurry..."

He yanked open the window, cool night air rushing into the room. With careful hands, he guided Lyric onto the metal fire escape outside. The cold steel bit into her palms as she gripped the railing.

The night embraced her as she stepped outside, her body adjusting to the precarious staircase clinging to the building's exterior. She began descending, the metal steps resonating softly beneath her weight.

Through a window offering a view of the elevator bank, something caught her attention, causing her to pause mid-step.

Inside, elevator doors parted with mechanical precision to reveal Governor Rada. She strode forward with purpose, heading toward her suite. Halfway across the lobby, she halted, her attention captured by movement beyond the window—a silhouette standing outside.

From Rada's perspective, this dark figure could have been anyone—man or woman—observing her from the shadows of night. Recognition dawned across Rada's face, replaced quickly by a cold fury that she barely contained.

With practiced composure, Rada swiped her keycard, unlocking her suite door. A final glance back revealed that the mysterious shape hastily descending the exterior staircase. Drawing a deep breath through flared nostrils, she fought to maintain her dignified façade while rage boiled underneath. The evidence of Cal's extra-extra-curricular activities stood clear as constellations in a winter sky.

With jaw clenched tight enough to crack walnuts, Rada pushed through the door.

Inside, she prowled through her quarters with predatory grace. The once-pristine suite now resembled Cal's personal flop pad—a state she'd grown accustomed to despite her resentment. His casual disregard for propriety only fueled the anger smoldering inside her.

"Oh hey. About to hop in the shower." Cal stood near the bathroom doorway wearing nothing but a towel wrapped around his waist, his performance almost convincing. He moved toward the bathroom with affected nonchalance.

Rada scanned the room methodically, her eyes lingering on the partially open window. She moved about the space with deliberate casualness, searching for evidence of the lover she knew just fled.

"What've you been up to tonight?" Her voice carried the dangerous softness of a drawn blade.

"This n'that. Saying Hi to friends." Cal's response floated back from the bathroom.

"Was 'she' one of them?" Rada approached the window, pushing it wider. She leaned out, surveying the fire escape and surrounding area. Finding nothing immediate, she withdrew—much to Cal's visible relief.

"...One of who?" His attempt at innocence rang hollow.

"Your many, many friends on campus." Acid dripped from each syllable.

"Ah, hm.... Yep." The acknowledgment emerged reluctantly. Caught in his deceit, Cal's demeanor shifted to brusque efficiency as he retreated into the bathroom.

The harsh fluorescent light illuminated white tiles as Cal turned on the shower. Steam began to rise, fogging the mirror as he tested the water temperature with outstretched fingers.

Rada positioned herself in the doorway, her unblinking stare boring into his back. Her rage rose dangerously close to boiling point.

"Who is this person?" Each word emerged precisely articulated.

"A friend." Cal didn't turn around.

"Name." The single word command hung in the humid air.

"...Chan Power." He repeated Lyric's pseudonym without hesitation.

"Do I know her?"

"Doubt it."

Fury propelled Rada back into the bedroom, where an unfamiliar item caught her attention. On the bureau sat something out of place—something not hers. Her fingers closed around the canvas handles of the feminist "Nevertheless She Persisted" tote bag.

"What is this?" She hoisted it up, feeling the weight of a bottle inside.

"Want it? It's yours. Have at it." Cal's voice carried from the bathroom.

"Everything in here is mine." The declaration resonated with ownership and betrayal.

Cal emerged to stand in the bathroom doorway, steam billowing around him. "Okay, Rada, talking like a slave owner—bad look for a Southerner."

"Don't try to be clever. You're not smart enough." Her voice dropped an octave.

"Smart enough to have you pinned-in pretty good." His smirk gleamed in the half-light.

"Fuck you." The words escaped through clenched teeth.

Cal moved toward the bed, bending to retrieve a discarded towel from the floor—one Lyric had used earlier. Before returning to the bathroom, he twisted the conversational knife deeper.

"Sometimes. But any mom in my class would be better in the sack than you."

He disappeared into the bathroom again, laying Lyric's towel on the floor outside the shower. Rada began to tremble, her composure cracking like thin ice.

Cal continued: "Are you really surprised I'd want to hook up with somebody younger?"

Rada followed him into the bathroom, still clutching the tote bag with white-knuckled intensity as Cal kept twisting:

"It'd be sad if you weren't so cruel—"

"Fuck you!" The words erupted from her core as she swung the canvas bag containing the whiskey bottle in a wide arc high up and onto Cal's head.

The impact produced a sickening crack. Cal collapsed instantly, motionless on the tile floor. Blood spurted from his skull in crimson pulses, mingling with steam from the shower and pooling across the white tile.

Rada remained frozen above him, the tote bag dripping whiskey onto the floor through the bag.

She caught sight of herself in the mirror—a stranger gazed back with wide, shocked eyes.

As reality seeped back into her consciousness, shock gave way to creeping fear. The bag slipped from her nerveless fingers, landing with a wet thud beside Cal's unmoving form.

***

The night air carried a chill as Rada stood on the doorstep of David's townhouse. Her face appeared raw from crying, eyes swollen and cheeks blotchy. Her trembling knuckles rapped against the solid wood door with desperate urgency.

David opened it wearing a bathrobe, his expression shifting from annoyed to bewildered as he recognized his late-night visitor.

"Governor. What...?" Confusion rendered him momentarily speechless.

"I need you to help me." Her voice cracked under the weight of her situation.

David noticed Emory, the young African American SUV driver peering curiously from the gubernatorial vehicle. With a dismissive wave, he silently commanded the young man's discretion. Emory's puzzled expression spoke volumes about the oddity of the governor's distressed appearance at David's residence.

David pulled Rada inside, shutting the door firmly against the night and whatever secrets it now held.

SUNDAY MORNING

Quiet like a held breath, the Southern Village Green lay dormant in the early morning light, a tableau of stillness punctuated only by the occasional rustle of blown leaves.

Inside the Stand Strong PAC offices, a different energy crackled through the air, electric with tension and unspoken fears.

Governor Rada's large office suite buzzed with hushed urgency. The sinister politician paced like a caged tigress, her pounding heels clicking a staccato rhythm against the polished hardwood. Conniving David perched on the edge of a chair, his eyes never leaving Rada's restless form.

He reassured her of the plan: "You said your State Police Captain, your whole protective detail, are all handpicked, they owe you. So you own them. This will work," David stressed, his voice low and conspiratorial.

Rada halted her pacing, fixing David with a piercing stare. "Look, I need you to steer them... away from certain things about Cal."

The unspoken hung between them—her sexual dalliances with her dead office boy toy Cal, the lover she had accidentally killed last night. David's knowledge of her affair bound him to her predicament like chains of complicity.

"The whole manhunt idea is to draw focus away from you. To anywhere else—" David's words trailed off as he watched conflicting emotions play across Rada's face.

"Right. You could say this 'Chan Power' person is a climate change radical." Rada's voice lowered to a whisper, conspiratorial and dangerous. "If you say they tried to kill me, the Party will rally to defend me."

David recognized her intention—to ensnare their entire political party and authority figures in this fabrication. His stomach coiled into knots. He ran anxious fingers through his hair, disturbing his otherwise impeccable appearance. His worry mounted with each breath.

"I'm not comfortable telling police—" The protest died on his lips as Rada cut him off.

"We'd both be lying to the police. And you work for me -- right, David?" The question carried no interrogative quality—it was a statement, a reminder of hierarchy and obligation.

David nodded, a shallow dip of his chin. His acquiescence sealed their pact.

Rada perched on the edge of her desk, close enough for David to smell her expensive perfume. Desperation clung to him like a second skin as his mind scrambled for alternatives. A memory surfaced—salvation in human form. He had arranged for his former co-worker Lyric to discuss potentially joining Rada's embryonic campaign.

"Lyric!" The name burst from his lips with renewed vigor. "Lyric only knows what we tell her. If we do keep the investigation in-house, but Lyric is our front; Lyric runs the search for Chan Power—so any blowback is on her." His words tumbled forth, gathering momentum. "And: she doesn't even work for the campaign!"

Their eyes locked in mutual recognition of opportunity. Smiles—slight, cautious, but unmistakable—crept across their faces. The elegant simplicity of using Lyric as their unwitting scapegoat appealed to them both. She would be their shield, their sacrifice if necessary, while they remained unscathed by the consequences of their deception.

In the golden morning light streaming through the tall windows, two political animals found common ground in self-preservation—willing to sacrifice an innocent to save themselves from drowning in the aftermath of violence and passion gone awry.

The morning light spilled through the wide windows of Luna Cafe, casting long rectangles across the polished wooden floor. Lyric shifted her weight from one foot to the other in the queue, her travel-worn jeans comfortable yet presentable enough for the flight home. Her rolling luggage stood sentinel beside her, packed and ready for departure. The smell of freshly ground coffee beans permeated the air, mingling with the warm scent of pastries.

Beside her, Mira—young, eager, with eyes bright with ambition—gazed at the menu board. Lyric had taken the aspiring journalist under her wing, recognizing in her a raw talent which reminded Lyric of herself a decade ago. Before the compromises. Before the disappointments.

Lyric's grip tightened around her copy of *The Washington Journal*, the disappointing newspaper that she'd given years of her life to. The headline screamed across the page in bold, accusatory type: "New Scrutiny Over Senator Nordström Endorsement Bribery." The weasel words sat like stones in her gut.

"Bullshit," she muttered, the word slipping out before she could catch it. "Tae-sung, coward. Goddamn."

Mira glanced at her, concern etching lines between her brows.

Lyric read the lede paragraph. Tae-sung had dumped her meticulously researched, triple-sourced investigation in order to run this sensationalist drivel. Her editor had caved to owner pressure again, printing a poorly-sourced hit-piece which would help a politician like Rada by muddying the waters of truth.

Her phone buzzed in her pocket. She fished it out, the screen illuminating with a message from David P:

Where are you!?

The digital exclamation points seemed to pulse with David's characteristic panic. Always demanding, always urgent, never actually important. Lyric's thumb hovered over the keyboard, but she slipped the phone back into her pocket without replying. David could wait. He always did.

She turned to Mira instead, forcing a smile. "I <u>am</u> going to get you a job. Maybe not at *The Journal*, though."

The words tasted bitter. She'd promised Mira an introduction, a foot in the door. But what kind of mentor would she be, leading another bright young woman into a newsroom governed by fear and capitulation?

A chirp from Mira's phone interrupted her thoughts. The younger woman's face changed as she read her own message, her expression shifting from curiosity to confusion.

"That's weird," Mira murmured, turning her screen toward Lyric.

Before Lyric could read it, her own phone rang. The screen displayed "Gov Rada" with a clarity which made her stomach drop. What could this be?

Lyric answered, her voice steadier than she expected. "Governor?"

The voice on the other end spoke rapidly, words tumbling over each other with uncharacteristic urgency. Lyric's spine straightened, her body tensing.

"Coming," she said, ending the call.

The cafe door swung open, admitting a gust of cool morning air – and a State Police officer. His uniform was crisp, his posture rigid. He scanned the room with practiced efficiency before his gaze locked onto Lyric. Their eyes met across the crowded cafe—his professional, hers apprehensive.

She knew in her bones something was very wrong. The unanswered text from David, Mira's strange message, the Governor's call, and now this—pieces of a puzzle assembling into an urgent picture she couldn't quite make out yet.

The barista called for the next customer. But Lyric stood frozen, luggage at her side as the officer moved toward her through the morning crowd.

***

The narrow passage between buildings funneled the morning breeze into a sharp wind as Lyric hurried after the State Trooper. Her rolling luggage bumped and skittered over the ground behind her, forcing her to yank it forward with increasing frustration.

The officer never once looked back, his long stride measured and mechanical. They approached one of the heavy metal doors at the rear of the main building—utilitarian, painted a dull gray, unmarked.

The door groaned open, revealing a staircase crossing upward through the clock tower. Cement and steel echoed under their feet. Light filtered through small dusty windows at regular intervals along the ascent, casting elongated rectangles across their path.

Lyric's breath came in short gasps as she raced to keep pace. Her luggage became heavy. The staircase yawned above her, airy and intimidating in its emptiness. The strain in her arms intensified with every floor they climbed.

At the second floor landing, another door awaited—this one marked with the Stand Strong PAC logo, a small bumper sticker affixed at eye level. The officer pushed it open without ceremony and gestured for her to enter.

Lyric emerged at the end of the bullpen near all the main offices. The officer walked Lyric over to Governor Rada's office suite door and knocked. He opened the door for Lyric to go through.

The Trooper shut the door behind Lyric with a soft click, leaving her alone with Rada and David.

They sat in matching leather armchairs, their postures mirroring one another—backs straight, hands clasped, faces carved into masks of concern. Lyric stood panting, her lungs burning from the climb, sweat prickling at her hairline. Her luggage listed sideways beside her, abandoned mid-roll.

Governor Rada broke the silence, her voice carrying across the room with authority. "Lyric, we have an emergency. A project only you can do. Only you. I will triple your yearly salary."

The offer hung in the air between them. Under different circumstances, such money might have tempted her. Lyric grimaced, her breathing still uneven. Her gaze flicked between Rada—whose political maneuvering had won her the top spot in her state—and David, whose snide remarks and calculating eyes had earned him the nickname "the weasel" among press corps veterans.

David leaned forward, his voice dropping into a register of false intimacy. "It is not opposition research. We believe there was an assassination attempt on the Governor last night."

The statement struck Lyric like a physical blow. Her eyes darted to Rada, searching for confirmation, for any hint of deception.

Rada intoned: "An anonymous call came in saying radical activists infiltrated the campaign with intent to kill." Rada's hands opening in a gesture of helplessness.

Lyric's mind raced. The timing seemed too convenient— suspiciously so. Only yesterday, in a moment of unguarded candor, Rada had expressed a wistful desire for confrontation with climate activists, for the political capital such conflict might generate. Now, here was her wish, gift-wrapped and delivered overnight.

"And now, we're unable to locate Cal," Rada added.

The world tilted beneath Lyric's feet. Cal—whose smile had begun to occupy her thoughts at odd moments, whose voice lingered in her memory long after their conversations ended. Gone? When she saw him last night there was no sign of him leaving, only an unspoken promise that he would be one to stay.

"We searched, called him; gone," David continued, his voice cutting through her thoughts. "This investigation needs to be handled in a politically astute manner, by the best investigator I know..."

"You, Lyric," Rada concluded. "Lives are on the line."

Lyric found her voice at last. "But. I'm not police. I wouldn't even know where to start."

"Start by finding 'Chan Power,'" Rada replied.

The pseudonym pierced Lyric's confusion like an arrow. She had shared it with Cal during a private moment—a joke between them, a bit of wordplay that burnished her indie rock bona fides. How could Rada know the fake name unless Cal told Rada about this for some reason?

"She—or he—was sighted last night," David added.

Lyric couldn't mask her confusion. Something was wrong. Deeply wrong. She was being manipulated, pushed onto a track not of her choosing, but who was behind it? Cal himself? These two political operators before her? Someone else entirely?

"You'll have the help of the State Police crew here on the Governor's guard assignment," David continued, "but no outside law enforcement, no Feds, no Press."

The Governor rose in one fluid motion and moved toward the door, gesturing for Lyric to follow.

The bullpen beyond Rada's office hummed with controlled tension. What should have been a space filled with campaign workers hunched over computers was only a crowd of uniformed State Police officers. They stood at attention, notepads and pens in hand, eyes forward, waiting. The sight chilled Lyric to her core—not an investigation team – but an army.

David emerged from the office last, closing the door with practiced precision. Lyric sensed him behind her, completing the circle of bodies. She was surrounded.

"These men are at your disposal to find Cal, and the terrorist Chan," Rada announced, her voice carrying across the silent bullpen.

David stepped forward toward the Governor's state police crew. "I suggest y'all go store-to-store asking for descriptions of anybody new seen talking with campaign staff."

The words sent ice through Lyric's veins. She was new here—a stranger in town. She fit the very description they would be hunting.

"Cal might have been a mole," Rada added, her expression grave.

"Uh? Where is Cal?" Lyric asked, still bewildered, still reeling, her voice smaller than intended.

"Exactly! And Chan Power," David replied, the non-answer hanging in the air.

He turned to the assembled officers with practiced authority. "Let us know when you find something."

A single clap echoed through the bullpen. The State Trooper Captain—a weathered man whose face seemed carved from granite—nodded to his men. They dispersed in perfect coordination, breaking into smaller groups, moving toward exits with military precision.

Lyric watched them go, panic rising in her chest. Whatever game was being played, she was neither a willing participant nor a knowing pawn.

"I'll...be right back," she managed, the words directed at Rada but spoken to no one in particular.

She darted across the bullpen toward the lobby, toward freedom, toward a moment to think. Her mind raced faster than her feet, connecting dots that formed no coherent picture.

Rada and David retreated back into Rada's office where he closed her door.

David settled into a calm demeanor, the urgency of moments before evaporated like the morning's dew. Rada sank onto the couch, anxiety still etched in the lines around her eyes.

"This'll work," David said, satisfaction coloring his words. "Lyric as our front," he beamed.

"But Chan saw me go in there," Rada countered, voice taut with worry.

"If we don't find Chan, then *he* killed his accomplice: Cal," David explained with clinical detachment. "If we *do* find Chan, your Guards will shoot to kill."

Rada was not listening. "I'm not going to prison. Understand?" Rada's words sliced through the air, sharp as a blade.

David nodded, the gravity of her worries reflected in his eyes. "Absolutely."

"When do we go to the press?" Rada asked, already calculating the political capital to be gained.

"Not until we find Chan Power," David replied, finality in every syllable.

In the relative safety of the elevator, Lyric's thoughts raced. She had to find Cal, had to unravel this web of lies before it ensnared her completely.

Sweat beaded along her hairline despite the cool air pumping through the vents. She stood rigid inside the metal box, fingers drumming against her thigh as she willed the doors to open.

The elevator announced itself with a bright 'ding' — reminiscent of a ski race's starting tone—its cheerful sound at odds with Lyric's mounting panic.

When the doors slid open, she burst forward racing from the elevator bank toward the hallway of Corporate Housing Suites.

Reaching Room #13—Cal's bedroom—she grasped the metal doorknob and twisted. It refused to yield. Locked.

"Lyric..."

The soft voice from behind made her jolt. Her young, puckish friend Mira peered out from her doorway several rooms down the corridor. She beckoned with urgent gestures, her eyes darting nervously toward both ends of the hallway. Lyric abandoned Cal's door and hurried toward Mira's suite, slipping into the doorway vestibule where Mira whispered:

"Governor's Police wouldn't let me in the Office. David ordered me to work from my room. All the fundraiser guys are in the rooms here. What's wrong?"

Lyric squeezed past Mira into her suite, closing the door with a soft click. The room smelled of hotel shampoo and takeout coffee. Lyric pressed her palm against the door as if securing it against invasion, struggling to keep her voice below a shout.

"What did David tell you? Exactly?"

Mira crossed her arms, brow furrowing. "Uh. He asked if I knew of anybody having 'secret trysts' with Cal."

"Shit. What did you tell him???" Lyric's words emerged sharp as broken glass.

"Nothing. Anyone who's seen his yoga class wants to fuck him."

Relief washed over Lyric—temporary, fragile. Perhaps they remained unaware of her intimate connection to Cal on the night Governor Rada killed him. Her reprieve lasted mere seconds before Mira continued:

"I heard a perimeter got set up at the road. Are we safe?"

Safety seemed a foreign concept now. Lyric's mind raced through possibilities, none offering comfort. A low-boil panic simmered beneath her practiced composure.

"I think…I'm being framed…but I don't know…if they know…it's me—"

Confusion clouded Mira's face, her head tilting slightly as she tried to parse Lyric's fractured musings. Lyric grasped the door handle, pulling it open.

"I have to see. What… Wait."

She jogged away, leaving Mira watching her disappear down the corridor, concern etched across her youthful features.

Minutes later, Lyric stood before Room 15, the master suite—scene of the crime. She pounded her fist against the solid wood, the thuds echoing through the empty hallway. Again, a locked door mocked her efforts. With a frustrated grunt, she spun and sprinted away.

The scheduling office appeared empty when Lyric slipped inside, closing the door silently behind her. Her gaze immediately found the multi-sleeve key card holder mounted on Estelle's wall—the repository for bedroom access cards for the floor upstairs. Every slot gaped empty. Room 15 included. A profanity formed on her lips.

"Can I help you find something?"

The voice sent electricity down her spine. She whirled around to find David peering into the office, his snake-like presence materializing from nowhere. His eyes—calculating, suspicious—bored into her.

Fear threatened to paralyze her. Instead, she armored herself with anger, launching verbal flares to mask her vulnerability.

"Obviously I'm looking for Estelle!" The words snapped from her mouth.

David stepped fully into the doorway, blocking her exit. "If you have questions, ask me."

Lyric recognized her only defense lay in offense. She squared her shoulders and advanced toward him.

"I have a question: Am I running this investigation? Or should I get on a plane and leave?"

"If you need something—"

"I need Estelle." Lyric cut him off, her voice rising with each word. "I need people with areas of expertise who I can trust to work within those areas, without fucking up my job! Do you understand me? Now, did you send her upstairs, or does she live in a Townhouse?"

A muscle twitched in David's jaw. "Townhouse."

"Get her back! And have her call me!"

Lyric pushed past him, her shoulder brushing his as she strode into the hallway. She prayed her bluster-bluff had worked, conscious of his gaze burning into her retreating form. She was walking a tightrope, and one false step could send her plummeting into the abyss beneath her feet.

***

The elevator deposited her at the ground floor. She marched toward the main doors, intent on escape, when movement outside caught her attention. Through the glass, she spotted several of the Governor's loyal

State Policemen clustered on the sidewalk, deep i
conversation with the bookstore clerk—the same on
who had seen Lyric with Cal last night.

Her blood froze as she watched the clerk gesture with he
hand positioned near her shoulder—indicating someon
of Lyric's height. One officer scribbled in a notebook
nodding. The witness could identify her. Thi
transformed her from potential investigator to suspect.

A growl of frustration escaped her throat as she spun
around, intending to catch the elevator back upstairs—
too late. The doors sealed shut, called to the office floo
above. Panic propelled her through the back doors of the
ground floor lobby.

Outside, the morning air struck cold against her flushed
skin. Lyric sprinted toward the fire escape stairs—the
same metal structure she had descended last night while
fleeing Governor Rada's room. Her lungs burned as she
climbed, each step clanging beneath her weight like a
death knell.

At Rada's window, she paused, catching her breath
before carefully sliding it open. The glass moved silently
along its track. She slipped inside the governor's
bedroom, memories of last night's hasty departure
flashing through her mind. The room appeared different
now—tidier, as if erased of evidence.

"Cal..." His name escaped as a whisper, partly prayer,
partly lament.

She crept toward the bathroom where light spilled onto
the carpeted floor. Her heart hammered against her ribs
as she turned the corner to find—

Emptiness. No one there.

Emboldened, she moved further into the pristine space, eyes cataloging details with forensic precision: water droplets beading on the tile floor; fresh towels folded on the vanity; tiny fragments of glass catching light from the overhead fixture. Bending closer, she discovered smears of blood on the door frame—crimson testimony to violence.

Back in the bedroom, Lyric surveyed the scene with mounting dread. The chair where Cal had piled his clothes now stood empty. The bureau where she had left her canvas tote bag was cleared, the bag vanished. But her green jacket—the one she'd draped over another chair during their intimate encounter—remained!

She snatched it up, stuffing the garment into a shiny plaid paper shopping bag she found nearby. With evidence in hand, she slipped out the door into the corridor. No master plan guided her movements—only the primal instinct for survival driving her forward as she improvised each desperate step.

The corporate housing hallway stretched before Lyric, fluorescent lights casting a sterile glow across the industrial carpet. She raced toward Room #13—Cal's bedroom—clutching the tall rectangular plaid shopping bag against her chest. Her footsteps echoed in the empty corridor, each sound a potential betrayal of her presence.

Outside his door, she pulled out her phone and dialed Cal's number. Pressing her ear against the cool wooden surface, she listened for any telltale ringing from within. Nothing but silence greeted her.

"Lyric?"

The voice from behind sent ice through her veins. David's tone carried false casualness, a predator's purr. She tucked the plaid shopping bag into Cal's door vestibule with practiced nonchalance before stepping out into the hallway.

Near the elevator bank stood David, accompanied by the State Police Captain—a monolithic figure whose presence commanded the space. Broad-shouldered and granite-faced, he exuded authority through stillness alone.

"Come here please..." David's words slithered across the distance between them.

After tucking the plaid shopping bag out of sight in Cal's door vestibule, Lyric moved toward the pair with measured steps, her body rigid, lungs refusing to expand. The distance between them diminished with excruciating slowness.

"Captain has a report..." David's eyes never left her face.

Lyric's gaze kept drifting to the Captain's holstered weapon. Dizziness threatened to overtake her. The police officer towered over her, his posture military-straight as he flipped open the cover of a small notebook.

"Troopers are compiling descriptions of everyone who was seen talking to campaign staff yesterday. Recurring details on 'Chan Power' are a green jacket and a canvas tote bag—"

"Excellent." The word escaped her lips while her mind screamed in horror. _Her_ green jacket, _her_ canvas tote. She stood before them, the very suspect they sought.

"And it's a woman," the Captain added, his expression unchanging.

Horror crashed through her. She stared at the Captain, willing her face to remain neutral while her mind raced. It was her word against everyone else's. She nodded slowly, as if thinking, buying precious seconds to compose herself.

David gestured down the hallway toward the bedrooms. "What are you doing?"

"Checking the rooms." Her voice emerged steadier than she expected.

"I already did. I have the master key."

David exchanged a glance with the Captain, a silent communication passing between them. He returned his attention to Lyric.

"Can we join you?"

David withdrew a key card from his coat pocket, holding it up as if presenting evidence. Beside him, the Captain patted his holstered gun, the gesture casual yet deliberate.

"Suspect's likely armed and dangerous, Miss. Lethal force is approved."

Lyric blinked at the weapon, her body instinctively recoiling. The possibility of violence hung in the air, tangible as smoke.

"Actually, it's fine—I've got it," David interjected. "You can go back to interviews."

The Captain straightened, professional courtesy overriding his desire to stay. "Sir. Miss." He nodded at each of them before turning toward the waiting elevator.

David strode toward Cal's room, Lyric following close behind. She cast a worried glance over her shoulder at the

Captain, who stood facing the elevator doors, his back to them.

Outside Cal's door, David's attention fixed on the plaid glossy paper shopping bag tucked along the wall.

"Is that yours? The governor had one—"

"It's a popular store," Lyric cut him off, extending her hand. "Key?"

David registered her interruption, filing it away for future reference. He handed over the room key card, his fingers brushing hers for a moment too long.

"Don't you worry."

His hand moved to the small of his back, retrieving a pistol with practiced ease. He held it up, mimicking the stance of a television detective. Lyric recoiled from the weapon, her breath catching.

"From the Governor's office safe," he explained, satisfaction evident in his tone.

Lyric inhaled deeply, centering herself. She managed a curt nod before sliding the key card into the lock. The mechanism clicked, granting them access.

Cal's room lay in darkness, the window open, allowing a breeze to disturb the curtains. Lyric inched forward, her eyes adjusting to the dim light. The comforter had been pulled from the bed, crumpled on the floor near the open bathroom door. The mechanical hum of the shower fan provided an eerie soundtrack to their intrusion.

David's fingers grazed her shoulder before he moved past her, positioning himself at the front. He advanced toward the bathroom, gun raised.

The sight within stole the breath from Lyric's lungs. Cal's naked body lay sprawled across the bathroom floor, blood-soaked towels scattered around him. Shards of broken glass glittered under the fluorescent light, tiny diamonds of destruction.

Lyric staggered backward, blinking hard against the image burning into her retinas. She forced herself to look again, to bear witness to the violence she had narrowly escaped.

From the trash can, David extracted a familiar item—her canvas tote bag.

"This is sold at that Always 21 store."

A grunt of acknowledgment was all Lyric could manage. Her eyes refused to stay fixed on Cal's corpse. She fought for breath, for composure, for any semblance of control as tears threatened to overwhelm her.

"You should remain running point," David continued, his voice distant through the roaring in her ears. "This is even more sensitive than ever. This Chan person was seen sneaking down the fire escape last night."

"Do...do we know what she looked like?" Lyric managed to form the words, each one a struggle.

"Troopers are talking to witnesses."

Sweat beaded on her forehead as she processed the cascade of revelations. Her breathing came in short, shallow gasps.

"Okay." The single word carried the weight of mountains.

"Do you want to tell the Governor?" David asked, his tone suggesting it was more command than question.

Lyric wiped away tears with the back of her hand, swallowing hard. Survival instinct pushed through her shock, demanding action.

"Uh. Yah. Let's go. Leave that." She pointed at the feminist canvas tote bag—her bag—now evidence in a murder investigation.

David returned it to the trash can before following her out of the room, leaving Cal's body behind them—a weight they now shared, a burden they carried differently.

DEAD

The air in Governor Rada's expansive office suite crackled with tension as Lyric stood before her, shoulders squared but spirit crumbling.

Lyric's heart fractured as she faced the cold, aloof Governor Rada. Grief and terror swirled within Lyric as she forced herself to maintain composure. David sat off to the side, a spider observing from its web, watching the interaction with calculated interest.

"Cal is…" Lyric's voice caught, the words sticking in her throat like shards of glass. "Dead. He's dead."

Governor Rada's face remained impassive, a political mask perfected through years of practice. "And the killer? Where is Chan?"

The lack of reaction struck Lyric like a phantom punch. No shock, no grief, no humanity in response to news of Cal's death. This sobering realization shifted something fundamental in her understanding of the situation.

"Caleb is dead, Ma'am," Lyric repeated, searching for any flicker of emotion across Rada's aristocratic jawline.

"The Governor served in Iraq," David interjected smoothly. "The Governor is cool in a crisis."

Lyric's eyes narrowed almost imperceptibly, her suspicions crystallizing into certainty. A sharp knock at the door interrupted the moment.

She crossed the plush carpet and opened the door to find the State Trooper Captain, his uniform crisp, his expression granite. His eyes locked onto Lyric, who fought to keep her breathing measured.

"Miss. The assassination threat likely came from somebody who had a romantic involvement with Cal Druck."

Governor Rada shifted in her chair, the first sign of genuine interest. "Really? Why do you say that?"

"A witness said Cal was on a date with a woman and they were talking about you, Ma'am."

"Me?" Rada's eyebrows arched. "So Cal was in on it."

David seized on this new narrative thread, recognizing its value in bolstering their fabricated alibi. "He could have helped Chan get access to the building. And things somehow went south?"

Terror surged through Lyric's veins, impossible to conceal. Every piece of evidence pointed directly at her. She teetered on the brink of complete panic, her body rigid with the effort to contain it.

"I'm curious what the witness overheard," Rada mused. "Thank you, Captain."

The State Trooper exited, pulling the heavy door closed behind him. In the subsequent silence, David turned to Lyric.

"You didn't tell him about Cal's body."

Rada nodded approvingly. "We are handling this completely in-house. No coroner yet. Smart."

Accepting the compliment with a slight nod, Lyric paced away from them both, desperately attempting to clear her mind of the fog of fear. Her thoughts scattered like leaves in a windstorm as she struggled to establish some semblance of control.

"We're gonna be okay," Rada remarked to David, a smile spreading across her face.

David returned the gesture with a conspiratorial wink, nodding obsequiously. His eagerness to please reminded Lyric of a trained dog performing for treats. "That bag... Killer's a liberal woman. We'll find out from the stores who bought that bag and the bottle."

His excitement at the prospect of Rada escaping consequences for Cal's murder radiated from him in sickening waves.

Lyric gazed out the window at people crossing the grounds below. Any one of those strangers could have witnessed her with Cal, could be providing a statement at this very moment. The walls of Rada's office seemed to contract around her, the oxygen thinning.

She turned to face Rada and David, who watched her with expectant expressions. Were they waiting for her to beg? To collapse? To confess?

"Do not reveal our evidence. Yet." Lyric's voice emerged stronger than she expected. She directed her next question to Rada: "Do you have a hair tie?"

"Excuse me?" Incredulity colored the Governor's response.

"I need to—focus."

Lyric pulled her hair into a tight ponytail, her fingers moving with purpose despite the tremor running through them. On a nearby shelf, she spotted a small knitted red beanie with "STAND STRONG" emblazoned across the front.

"Can I borrow this?"

At Rada's nod, Lyric tucked her hair up inside the hat, a small disguise but better than nothing. She cracked her neck—a performance of preparation masking desperate improvisation.

"Cal. Let's follow up on Cal," she said, grasping for a strategy to redirect attention. "What was he up to? Why would he turn on you? Why was he naked?"

Before either could respond, Lyric moved toward the door, intent on shifting the investigation away from "Chan" and toward Cal himself.

"Wait, I'm not sure that's—" Rada began, but Lyric had already vanished into the hallway.

Rada and David scrambled after her, exchanging worried glances as they pursued her into the main building's office bullpen.

The large open workspace buzzed with subdued activity. Several State Police officers stood with the Captain, awaiting instructions. Lyric seized the opportunity to take command.

"Everyone! Gentlemen! Listen up!"

Estelle emerged from her scheduling office, clipboard in hand. Lyric launched into an offensive strategy:

"Estelle, I need a printout of Cal Druck's documents. 1099, W-4, his application, everything."

Behind her, David and Rada exchanged subtle glances of concern, their unspoken communication louder than words.

"Captain, look at his bank statements," Lyric continued, her voice carrying across the space.

"To see what he and Chan Power did together?" David inserted himself into the conversation, attempting to regain control.

"Estelle, do we have his computer? Passwords?" Lyric pressed forward.

"I can look." Estelle's brow furrowed. "Do we know where he is?"

Lyric glared at David, her expression conveying her desire to tell Estelle the truth. David stepped in swiftly:

"Not yet. We're already gathering security video from the stores where we know they went together."

A smile stretched across Lyric's face—a rictus of fear as her inner voice screamed in panic, *We are?!*

"Roadblocks continue," Rada announced with gubernatorial authority. "Nobody in or out without checking IDs."

"We find Chan," David concluded. "You have Lyric's orders."

The troopers dispersed, filing out of the bullpen. Estelle retreated to her office, leaving Lyric alone with David and Rada. Too many players now controlled this investigation, each with their own agenda. Irritation flared as Lyric turned on David before he could escape with Rada.

"Hey—Tell me about the security video 'we're already gathering'...?"

David's response came without hesitation. "The mall's surveillance cameras are encrypted. So we'll need to use the security firm to render the video."

"No!" Lyric's voice grew sharp. "I can render any video...codec, deinterlaced without contacting the company. No leaks! Jesus, David."

Rada's eyebrows rose, clearly impressed. Neither she nor David understood the technical jargon—but neither did Lyric. Another desperate bluff in a game growing more dangerous by the minute.

"I'll do it. I'll get my computer." Lyric jogged away from them, leaving them staring after her with impressed expressions, buying herself precious moments alone to pull a thorn from her side.

In the rear of the main building, in the shade, Lyric stood before an industrial dumpster, its metal lid propped open against her shoulder. A breeze ruffled her hair while she extracted an envelope of cash from her green jacket—the envelope labeled, "Lyric" in David's unmistakable handwriting.

She pocketed the envelope and tossed the jacket into the garbage bin's dark maw and released the lid. It crashed down with a sharp, echoing bang which ricocheted off the surrounding buildings. Lyric winced.

Four doors down, the sound drew attention… A chubby man with cigarette smoke curling around his face leaned out from the back door of the Print Shop whose branded smock he wore. His eyes narrowed as he peered up the walkway, focusing on Lyric's slender form.

Oblivious to his scrutiny, Lyric reached into her pocket and pulled out a plaid glossy shopping bag. She lifted the dumpster lid again—this time with greater care—and deposited the bag inside before easing the lid shut with barely a whisper of black plastic against metal.

Her eyes darted around the parking lot as she hurried back up toward the Governor's office building, her footsteps quick and light against the pavement.

***

Later, in the sanctuary of Mira's room number 10, Mira perched on the edge of her neatly-made bed. The blinds, closed by Lyric limited daylight to slight stripes across the sparse furnishings. Lyric occupied the room's only chair, her body coiled with tension, hands gripping her knees.

"You need to know: The Governor was sleeping with Cal." Lyric's voice remained steady despite the bombshell she'd dropped.

Mira absorbed nonchalantly, a flicker of recognition crossed her face, but no shock. She'd seen too much in her short time here.

"He told me he hooked up with you," Mira replied, her voice measured.

Lyric's composure faltered. "Shit." She leaned forward, desperation evident in every line of her body. "I need your help. My word is not enough versus all the..." She paused, searching for words. "I need proof it wasn't me. I need evidence."

"What the hell is happening?" Mira's question drew a line in the still air between them. Lyric needed to entrust Mira.

Lyric pressed a finger against her right eye, which had begun to vibrate involuntarily. She swallowed hard, fighting against a sob rising in her throat.

"Last night..." She paused, gathering courage. "Cal—Cal is dead and it looks like I did it."

Shock transformed Mira's face. Her mouth opened and closed several times, words failing her as the implications caromed through her mind. Lyric lunged forward, grabbing Mira's hand in both of hers, the contact almost desperate.

"I didn't! But you can't tell anybody. And you don't know. Please! Help me. I'm in serious danger." Her fingers tightened around Mira's.

"Oh my God. What?!" Mira's voice rose an octave, panic bleeding through.

"I need you to help me, Mira." Lyric's eyes never left the younger woman's face. Mira could not compute how she could possible help such a disastrous mess.

"How am—Okay?" Mira stammered, her breathing shallow. "Oh my God..."

Lyric's mind raced ahead, formulating plans, discarding options. "Whaddya know about rendering video?"

"Nothing. What??" Confusion wrinkled Mira's brow.

A smile ghosted across Lyric's face. "Good, me neither, this'll take as long as it takes. That's good."

"What am I doing???" Mira pulled her hand away, rubbing her sweating palm against her jeans.

Lyric stood up, energy renewed with purpose. "You're buying me time. New plan." She reached for Mira's reluctant hand again, her fingers cool against the younger woman's warm skin. They had work to do.

***

Lyric sat at Mira's computer slightly confused, her fingers trembling as she plugged in the rubber orange hard drive David had handed her. Mira stood off to the side, having an out-of-body experience.

"This is the stores, over in the mall," David explained, hovering close enough for Lyric to catch his coffee breath.

Lyric nodded, not looking up from the screen. "Mira will be here to deinterlace on the fly while we work. Right?"

Mira startled at being addressed. "...Yup," she affirmed, her voice disguising uncertainty.

David shifted his weight towards Mira. "How long will it take?"

Mira's eyes darted toward Lyric, silently pleading for rescue from the question she couldn't answer.

Lyric's fingers hovered over the keyboard. "Give me a sec. It's gotta import." Fear flickered across her face, visible only to Mira who stood at the right angle to see it.

On the monitor, a progress bar crawled forward with excruciating slowness.

A knock interrupted the tense silence. An anxious and thin state cop with darting eyes entered without waiting for permission and crossed directly to David. He leaned in close, whispering urgently into David's ear. David's eyebrows shot up as he listened.

Lyric watched this exchange, her heart hammering against her ribs. "Guys, I'll get you an estimate when it's ready. Is there something you need from me? Can we get to work?"

David hesitated, then shrugged—a gesture of apparent acquiescence. "No problem," he muttered before he and the officer stepped away. The officer glanced back at Lyric once as they left.

Lyric remained frozen until they disappeared through the doorway. She rose from her chair in one fluid motion and closed the door with a soft click. Returning to the computer, she opened a browser and typed rapidly: "How do I convert—"

Reading over Lyric's shoulder, Mira could see the slog ahead: "Oh, man." Mira's voice carried frustrating disbelief.

"Please take over," Lyric requested, vacating the chair. "Once you figure out how to do it, <u>don't</u>. Find me first."

Mira slid into the seat, her fingers hovering uncertainly over the keyboard.

"As far as you know, Cal's 'missing.' That's all." Lyric's voice dropped to a near-whisper.

"What the hell." Mira glanced up at her. "Who d'ya think did it?"

Lyric shook her head, her face tightening. "I can't say—without proof. I need someone who saw..." Her words tumbled faster. "Um... The Black SUVs! How do you call a ride?"

Outside David's office, the thin state cop guided David toward his door with barely concealed urgency.

The officer's youthful face betrayed anxiety despite attempts at professional detachment. Standing beside David's door was the Print Shop clerk, the smoker, clutching the plaid shopping bag in hands.

Both the officer and David glanced back toward Mira's closed door, suspicion hardening their features. David pushed his door open with unnecessary force.

"Inside," he commanded, his voice clipped.

Sunlight bounced off the polished black exterior of an SUV as Ty guided it into a loading zone near the Lobby Door of the main building.

From across the way, through the large windows of the campus café, movement caught the eyes of patrons—Lyric rushed toward the parked SUV, her head bowed low as if to avoid recognition. Her path took her directly to the passenger side of Ty's vehicle.

Inside the parked SUV, the morning's treatment of leather conditioner still perfumed the air. Ty's kind eyes smiled broadly to see Lyric again as she slipped into the passenger seat, her breathing rapid from her dash from the elevator lobby.

"Ty. Is there any way off campus without showing my ID?" The words tumbled from her lips, urgent and breathless.

Ty's smile dimmed slightly. "No, Miss Lyric. It's closed up tight." His voice carried the gentle cadence of his Georgia upbringing.

Lyric's shoulders dropped momentarily before she rallied. "OK. How can I get a record of rides you guys made last night? To here, or from here. But without raising alarms? At 1 AM, 1:30? -ish."

"That'd be the night crew." Ty's fingers drummed once against the steering wheel. "A young brother, Emory, I think drove." His eyes met hers. "I'm guessing you want his number?"

Lyric nodded vigorously, hope flaring in her eyes.

With unhurried movements that attempted to calm the tension in the air, Ty reached up to his sun visor and retrieved a small, dog-eared company brochure. His warm smile never wavered as he located the information she sought.

ALL IS LOST

The noon sun filtered through the half-drawn blinds of David's office, casting prison-bar shadows across his desk. David sat behind it, a vibrating, coiled serpent waiting to strike. His unseen heel tapped an anxious rhythm against the carpet—a metronome counting along with the racing of his thoughts. Though his face remained composed, his eyes betrayed him, darting out to the people in his room, always returning to the tall plaid shopping bag resting on his desk.

Across from him stood the witness in a faded Copy Store smock, the acrid scent of cigarettes clinging to his clothes. David listened with feigned attentiveness, his mind racing through scenarios, possibilities, consequences—a chess player planning ten moves ahead.

"She had your campaign hat on, all scared, an' I hadn't seen her before, so when y'all came askin' if anybody with a bag was hanging 'round—" The Copy Store clerk's voice grated with the rasp of too many cigarettes.

David interrupted, gesturing toward the bag. "But that's not canvas."

The wiry State Cop whose perpetual anxiety manifested in a constant shifting of weight from one foot to another—reached into the plaid shopping bag. He extracted a green jacket with a frustrated urgency.

"What about the jacket?" The cop's voice rose involuntarily. Standing beside the Copy Store clerk, it was them two vs one.

David maintained his composure, a mask of professional concern hiding the calculation beneath. He needed to protect Lyric—but for what purpose…

"Wasn't in the bag, right?" David raised an eyebrow.

The State Cop shook his head no.

"Right. But thank you for your help…But, um, this-this was the Governor's bag, and I— we told Lyric to toss it." David's voice remained steady, a practiced performance. Unsurprisingly, the political monster lied well.

The Anxious Statie gestured toward the green jacket again, his expression questioning.

David nodded, conceding the smallest point to maintain control of the larger narrative. "Yes, it might be the jacket. So…you can leave that inside there. I'll follow up with Lyric, but, yes, the search continues. Good work. Thanks again for coming in."

"Sir." The Statie's acknowledgment carried the responsibility of military discipline.

"Okay." The smoker nodded, shrugging, relieved to be dismissed.

The Anxious Statie opened the door, a courteous gesture for the Copy Store clerk. When the door clicked shut,

David exhaled. His shoulders dropped a fraction of an inch—the only sign of relief he allowed himself.

With practiced smoothness, he took the tall plaid bag and rolled his chair back, tucking it into the kneehole under his desk. He leaned back, his heel resuming its rapid tapping against the carpet. His fingers traveled to the corner of his mouth, scratching at the beginning of a cold sore. His mind raced through permutations and combinations, weighing risks against rewards, paths to power against potential pitfalls.

In the main bullpen beyond David's office, the anxious State Cop opened the back door for the smoker. They exited toward the rear stairwell, the door slowly swinging shut behind them.

At that precise moment, Lyric ran from the distant elevators through the empty bullpen. She carried her phone, her gaze fixed on Mira's room as she ran.

The door to Mira's spacious group office swung open as Lyric rushed in, closing it behind her with urgency. The room hummed with the quiet whir of the external hard drive spinning.

Mira looked up from her workstation, a flash of excitement crossing her face. "Got it working! It'll take 20 minutes—"

"Nonononono, longer! How can..." Lyric interrupted, breathless and desperate. She dropped into one of the many unused office chairs at empty workstations.

Mira quickly offered back: "Higher quality video takes longer," anticipating Lyric's needs.

"Good, OK, do it higher. Adjust it. I need longer. Figure it out." Lyric's words tumbled out, each one pushing against the next.

"Roger." Mira nodded, focus returning to her screen.

Lyric rolled her chair away, reaching for a nearby landline. She punched in numbers scanning the text on her phone screen.

"Hi. Stand Strong PAC here..." She spoke into the receiver, her voice shifting into professional mode. "The number I have for one of your drivers, Emory, isn't working—"

She paused, listening. Her expression darkened. "...Oh." The confusion hidden in her voice drew Mira's attention. "When? And do you know where?" Lyric continued.

The click of the call ending echoed in her ear. She stared at the phone, stunned to be hung up on. Mira turned to face Lyric.

Lyric relayed with disbelief the cover story: "He went on an 'island vacation' - this morning. They're getting rid of him." Lyric's voice dropped to a whisper, fear seeping into every syllable. The implication hung heavy in the air: Cal's killer would eliminate anyone who might expose them.

"What island?" Mira asked, her fingers hovering above her keyboard.

Lyric shook her head. No, she didn't know. But memory sparked in her eyes as she recalled Cal's words from the previous day: "Hilton Head, Antigua, Bermuda..."

Revelation dawned across her face. She bolted from her chair and rushed out of Mira's office, moving with renewed purpose.

The scheduling office sat quiet and organized, a stark contrast to Lyric's chaotic energy as she burst through the door. Estelle looked up from her desk, her expression unreadable.

"David booked a retreat for us to go to Hilton Head, right?" Lyric asked, her voice tight with urgency.

Estelle nodded without emotion. "Some of us. Correct." She had not been invited.

"How can I contact the airport people?"

"That's Mister Waylos's jet. I'd ask the Governor." Estelle's tone remained neutral, professional.

Lyric flashed a double thumbs-up, spinning toward the door. But she harbored no intention of approaching Governor Rada Waylos—not when Rada might be Cal's killer.

In the main bullpen, Lyric collided with a State Cop heading toward David's office. Channeling the authoritative tone she'd heard David use countless times, she barked, "Report."

The cop straightened, responding to the command in her voice. "We found a witness who can identify Chan Power. She was seen on campus minutes ago."

Adrenaline surged through Lyric's veins, her mind racing to process this information. All signs pointed to "Chan Power" being used to describe her own actions.

"How do we know it's her?" Lyric asked, maintaining her composure through sheer force of will.

"This witness saw her at a Pilates class yesterday with Cal. And on the sidewalk just earlier today."

"Interesting. Okay, wait here." Lyric strode toward Rada's office, her heart pounding against her ribcage.

She knocked on the Governor's door, her knuckles rapping against the wood with more confidence than she felt.

"Come in," Rada's voice called from within.

The sound of the knock alerted David, who scurried quickly from his office. He followed Lyric as she stood in Rada's doorway, observing the scene from behind with calculating eyes.

Governor Rada sat behind her desk, the phone receiver nestled back into its cradle. Sunlight streamed through her large window, illuminating her relaxed posture. "What's up?" she asked, her voice light and musical.

"Chan Power was in a Pilates class with Cal," Lyric began, thinking quickly. "I think we should focus on the list of students at that Pilates school. And go one-by-one."

From behind Lyric, the State Cop interjected, correcting her strategic omission. "Ma'am, Chan Power is on campus now."

David pushed forward, his voice rising with alarm. "What?!"

"Where?!" Rada demanded, her relaxed demeanor vanishing.

"Should I bring the witness here?" the cop asked.

Lyric moved quickly, desperate to prevent a confrontation with someone who might identify her. "No, no - Let's not draw too much attention to the Governor."

"Good point," Rada agreed, oblivious to Lyric's true motivations.

David watched Lyric closely, his suspicion mounting with each passing second.

"Bring the witness around to high traffic areas on campus. Subtly..." Lyric instructed the cop, her mind racing for solutions.

"Good idea. Dismissed," Rada confirmed.

The State Cop nodded. "Yes, Ma'am. Miss." He departed, leaving tension hanging in the air like smoke.

"Inside. Close the door." Rada's voice hardened, the pleasant tone evaporating.

Lyric stepped into the office, fear coiling in her stomach. David followed, closing the door with a soft click that sounded like a prison cell locking.

Governor Rada Waylos leaned forward, her expression shifting to one of calculated strategy. "Time to talk Media strategy."

David's eyes remained fixed on Lyric, seeing through her façade. "The net is tightening, huh?" he quietly said to Lyric.

"Yeah," Lyric mumbled, avoiding his gaze.

When David moved closer, Lyric retreated to the window. Outside, the State Cop escorted a woman in yoga attire—the witness who could identify her—toward the crowded gazebo.

David moved to sit in in his leather chair beside Rada's desk.

"Once we catch the killer, we reveal the body," Rada continued, oblivious to the drama inside Lyric as she looked out Rada's window. "But we also need to show Chan's ties to radicals. What reporters do you have who'll play ball?"

Lyric remained transfixed by the scene outside, watching as the identification process began. She was not ready to engage on this machination yet. "Hm," she bluffed, "I'll have to think about this."

Lyric crossed the office toward the door, moving as if in a trance. David followed, his stride purposeful.

"We need to talk. Where are you going?" he demanded.

"Evidence is coming in." The lie slipped from Lyric's lips with ease.

"What...what evidence?" Rada's voice carried a hint of panic.

"Security footage from the elevators." Lyric maintained her composure, savoring the flicker of fear in Rada's eyes.

"Really?" David's skepticism was evident.

"Yep. Backup cameras." Lyric allowed herself a moment of satisfaction at their discomfort before exiting, leaving David and Rada to their shared anxiety.

Rada pointed at herself, her voice dropping to a whisper. "Elevator." The word hung in the air—a confession of her presence in the elevator the night she killed Cal.

In the main office bullpen, David rushed from Rada's office. Before Lyric could reach Mira's room, he called out, "Lyric! Dumpster-diving?"

Lyric slowed, processing his words. Before she could turn and respond, David grabbed her upper arm, his fingers digging into her flesh as he pulled her toward his office.

"Hey. Heyyy," she protested, her voice rising.

"You're out of time," David hissed, his breath hot against her ear.

Inside his office, David positioned himself against the closed door, blocking her escape. Lyric backed away, maintaining distance between them.

"I don't want to hurt you. I want to protect you." His voice softened, a predator adapting its approach.

Lyric maintained her innocence, her expression carefully neutral. David crossed to his desk and retrieved the plaid shopping bag from the floor. He placed it atop his desk with deliberate slowness, then pulled out her green jacket—evidence retrieved from the dumpster.

"You were seen. Just like you were seen outside the window last night." His voice carried a hint of triumph.

"That proves nothing." Lyric kept her voice steady, though her heart raced.

"But it looks really bad for you." David's lips curved into a smile devoid of warmth.

"I did nothing wrong. And you know it." Defiance blazed in her eyes.

"You feel this- this noose, tightening- I can help you out of this." He leaned forward, invading her space.

"Oh, really, how?" Skepticism dripped from every word.

"Work for me like we did before." The proposal hung in the air between them.

Lyric chuckled a huff. David mistook her reaction for doubt.

"I can keep you out of trouble." His voice dropped to a conspiratorial whisper.

"Exactly," Lyric mused. "This is exactly what Rada did to Cal. Golden handcuffs." Pained understanding dawned in her eyes.

David shrugged, to his cynical heart the world was nothing but handcuffs – golden ones were simply the best.

Lyric nodded. "...How? What would you do?" Lyric asked, buying time.

"I don't know yet. We'd figure it out." His casual tone sounded like an honest invitation to join his conspiratorial mindset.

"...Let me think about this." Stalling again, Lyric's mind raced, searching for escape.

"You can't run forever. Lyric—" David began, but she was already moving for his door.

Lyric fled his office, leaving David frustrated yet hopeful, unaware of the wheels turning in her mind as she plotted her next move in this dangerous game of chess.

THE PLAN

Lyric ducked into Mira's office, closing the door behind her with a soft click. Her shoulders rose and fell with a shaky breath, the adrenaline from her confrontation with David still coursing through her brain. The room hummed with the gentle whir of Mira's computer fan.

"I need a Hail Mary. Time estimate?" Lyric's voice cracked, betraying her desperation.

Mira glanced at her monitor, her face bathed in the blue glow. "39 minutes. Got another plan?"

Lyric collapsed into a chair, pulling out her phone. She stared at her phone screen, her mind racing through possibilities, discarding each one as quickly as it formed.

"No. Nope." Her mouth twitched—a nervous tic newly emerging under her stress.

"Damnit, no, that's not gonna work..." she muttered, more to herself than to Mira.

"Whuh?" Mira pivoted in her chair, fingers paused above her keyboard.

Lyric looked off into space working through the problem aloud: "Private airport, personal jet; probably wouldn't get info -- definitely would raise alarms. Nope." Lyric shook her head, dismissing the idea. The walls seemed to close in around her, options dwindling with each passing second.

In one fluid motion, she sprung from the chair and darted toward the door, leaving a dumbfounded Mira staring after her. The sound of the door opening and closing echoed in the room.

Estelle's scheduling office existed in a state of perpetual order—a stark contrast to the chaos unfolding around it. Lyric slid inside, closing the door behind her with practiced smoothness. Estelle sat behind her desk surprised, her eyes questioning.

"Do you have the numbers for building security? Both this building and all the governor's island properties?" Lyric asked, her voice steady despite the storm raging inside her.

Estelle nodded, rising from her chair. "I do. Right here."

She crossed to the wall, gesturing toward a printout of names and numbers. Lyric moved closer, pulling out her phone and snapping a photo of the list.

"I also need this building's security camera footage - from the elevators and hallways. Please give it to Mira?" Lyric tried to keep her tone casual, as if requesting nothing more significant than a coffee order.

"I'll call building security now." Estelle reached for her landline, her movements purposeful as if, perhaps, Estelle knew that Lyric was desperate for some larger assistance.

Lyric studied the printout on the wall, her eyes scanning the names and numbers. She entered one of the numbers into her phone but paused before pressing "call." With one last glance at Estelle – with thanks – she stepped outside the office.

The quiet of the main bullpen broke as the State Police Captain emerged from David's office, stopping short when he spotted Lyric.

"What is it?" Lyric asked. Whatever news he had just shared with David could not be allowed to stay secret.

The Captain held up a laptop adorned with a band's sticker. "David asked us to crack the vic's electronics. See who his most recent contacts were."

These would show that he'd been messaging with Lyric! "I...dunno, is that smart?" Lyric hedged, buying time as her mind processed this new liability.

"Governor said don't worry about warrants. Just, where should I send the phone data. What's your email?" The Captain asked.

"Send it to Mira. You found his phone?" Lyric asked, her eyes narrowing.

The Captain upturned his head, uncomfortable. "Miss… David did not want a large crew in on this."

Annoyance flashed across Lyric's face—another instance of being circumvented. She gestured for the Trooper Captain to follow her past Estelle's open door and into Mira's office.

Mira looked up as they entered, her expression shifting from surprise to wariness. Lyric stood in the doorway, the Captain hovering behind her.

"Mira, David and me were just in here with you a minute ago, talking about you processing the data, that right?" Lyric's voice carried a hint of urgency.

Mira blinked, confusion evident. "Yeah. Why?"

"Is that the computer that's processing the data?" Lyric pointed toward Mira's workstation.

After a moment's hesitation, Mira nodded yes.

."Great. Give me your business card." Lyric extended her hand, palm up.

Mira reached for her desk, retrieving a small, white card. She passed it to Lyric, who handed it to the State Police Captain.

"So, Captain. Please don't second-guess me. All that does is slow us down. Thank you..." Lyric's voice hardened. "You may go."

The Captain offered a small, reluctant nod before turning and exiting the room. The door closed behind him with a soft thud.

"What was that about?" Mira asked.

"When you get a weird email from him, lemme know. It's bad for me. How much longer on this?" Lyric moved closer to Mira's workstation, peering at the screen.

"I slowed it down as much as I can. There's 37 minutes left." Mira pointed to a progress bar crawling across the bottom of the screen.

Lyric pressed dial on her phone, tapping Mira's shoulder to get her attention. "I'm sending you a list of the Governor's properties, now watch--"

Her voice shifted, becoming chipper and professional as she spoke into the phone: "Hello, I'm calling from Governor Rada Waylos's Office. Just making sure Security has been alerted about our incoming guest. Has he arrived yet? It's just one passenger, an African American male, name: Emory."

She listened for a moment, her face falling slightly. "Ah. I must have the wrong location."

Lyric ended the call, her demeanor shifting once more as she turned to Mira. "So it's not Hilton Head. Can you go down the list and say what I said? I'll need the address and a direct contact number. Between you and me."

Mira gave a thumbs up, understanding the importance of the request. Lyric nodded back and exited the room.

The main bullpen stretched before her, a valley of empty cubicles and desks. Lyric emerged from Mira's room, only to stop short, crestfallen. Across the floor, the State Police entourage entered from the elevators, accompanied by the glum waiter from "Blue Ridge Distillery."

Simultaneously, Governor Rada and David emerged from Rada's office, their faces set in matching expressions of determination.

"The witness who heard something about me is here?" Rada's voice carried across the space, commanding attention.

Lyric turned her back to the approaching crowd and tapped her ear pod, holding up one finger in a "wait" gesture. Her mind raced, formulating a plan on the fly.

"I'm on with the reporter you told me to feed the cover story..." she improvised, her voice steady despite the panic rising in her chest.

"Great." Rada chirped back.

"No. Illegal. I can't be seen doing this. You have to cover for me." Lyric's plea included David, her eyes darting between them.

Rada nodded, accepting the excuse. With her path cleared, Lyric fled toward the back stairwell, her back turned always to the witness.

David watched her go, a glint of bemused impatience in his eyes. The chess pieces moved across the board, and he wondered what her next desperate move would be—unaware that she was playing a game of her own with maneuvers he could never comprehend: At the top of Lyric's task list was saving the life of Emory, a man who she had never met.

Lyric's footsteps echoed against the steel treads as she raced up the empty back staircase of the main building. Her lungs burned with each sharp intake of breath, but she pressed on, switch-backing higher away from the Governor's Office.

She continued climbing until she reached the highest point of the structure—the belfry. The so-called bell tower housed no actual bell, merely the architectural suggestion of one, another facade in a building full of lies.

At the top landing, Lyric halted, her pulse hammering in her throat. After checking that nothing stirred beneath her in the stairwell, she extracted her phone from her pocket. One, two rings sounded before the connection clicked open.

"I need Tae-sung," she commanded without preamble, her voice low but urgent.

After a moment, she heard Tae give his greeting and cut him off: "I have a situation—" She started then restarted; "I'm in Georgia, I need help; do we have a fixer down here who could pass for a reporter?"

As she listened to the response, her gaze drifted through the small, dingy glass toward the Village Green below— picnic blankets on the manicured lawn transformed it into a chessboard nearing endgame.

"Yes you <u>do</u> owe me," she countered, her tone demanding but grateful for acknowledgment of past efforts. Relief softened her features as the voice on the other end capitulated. "Okay, so first—"

The door to Governor Rada's office opened with a soft whoosh. A State Trooper emerged from inside, guiding the Blue Ridge Distillery's Glum Waiter out toward the elevators. As the pair disappeared down the bullpen aisle, the door swung shut again with a definitive click.

Inside her office, Governor Rada whirled to face David, her composure cracking like thin ice. "Who do you think it is?" she demanded, her voice pitched low but edged with panic.

David paced the Persian rug, his leather shoes sliding along the plush fibers with each turn. He forced an air of anxiety for her delight.

"I don't know," he said, running a hand across his balding pate. "But we have a more pressing matter: That driver."

Rada's jaw tightened. She crossed to her executive chair and sank into it, the leather creaking beneath her weight. "Don't worry about him. He's gone."

She spun away from David, presenting him with her back as she stared out the window. The Village Green stretched below. People moved about their morning routines, oblivious to the drama occurring above.

David continued his relentless pacing, his voice rising with each word. "He drove you to my house. He has to go! I don't—"

"I don't want anyone else hurt," Rada cut in, her fingers dug into the armrest. "The Driver's out of the picture."

"You can't guarantee that!" David exploded, jabbing a finger toward her. His face flushed crimson, veins bulging at his temples. "As soon as Lyric does her media magic—"

"—I'll have the whole Party's help," she finished, her voice hardening into steel.

"This Driver can ruin that! Ruin us!" David's voice cracked with desperation. A new thought struck him, widening his eyes. "Wait, were you and him also—"

"Stop! Stop this!!" Rada commanded, swiveling to face him.

They glared at each other across her oversized desk. The depth of their complicity hung between them, a shared secret turning rancid.

David drew a deep breath, regaining a veneer of control. "No loose ends. I'm sending the Captain—"

"I…" Rada began with a force she immediately surrendered. "I don't want to know," Rada murmured, turning away once more. The morning light caught her profile, throwing half her face into shadow.

She stared through the window, her gaze unfocused. "Where is Lyric?!"

A buzz alerted on Lyric's phone. She peeked at her screen: "come back 911." From Mira. The code for emergency.

Lyric pressed her phone back to her ear. "Tae, I gotta run. Hurry," she urged into the phone, her voice hushed yet urgent.

Lyric grimaced, ending the call with Tae. She shoved the phone into her pocket and quickened her pace, descending the stairs two at a time. Her footfalls echoed in the stairwell, a percussive accompaniment to her racing thoughts.

She reached the landing where the office entrance waited with whatever new crisis Mira had discovered. Lyric pushed through, emerging into the office bullpen.

Lyric slipped from the stairwell, her movements fast and silent across the office carpet. Adrenaline sharpening her senses, she reached Mira's office door. Lyric twisted the handle and slipped inside, closing the door behind her with a soft click.

Mira looked up as Lyric entered, relief washing over her features.

"What???" Lyric demanded, keeping her voice low.

Mira leaned forward, her words tumbling out in an urgent stream. "Estelle came looking for you—David's looking for you too—but Estelle said the security system guy called back—"

Lyric moved closer, her expression urging Mira to accelerate her explanation. Time was a luxury they lacked.

"He said this building's elevator camera footage got *taken*," Mira finished.

"Taken? When?" Lyric pressed, her mind racing through the implications.

"Six AM," Mira replied, her eyes wide. "Then the guy got sent home—by David. So he's been lying."

Anger flashed across Lyric's face, but surprise was notably absent. She knew David was not to be trusted.

"Super," she muttered, the word dripping with sarcasm. "What about the islands?"

Mira shook her head, frustration evident in her furrowed brow. "Still looking. It's not Antigua, not Barbados or…"

Lyric glanced at Mira's computer screen. There, in plain view, was the photo Lyric had taken of Rada's property list—names and numbers of offshore holdings, potential stash houses to hide someone…or hide their body.

"You've got to go faster," Lyric urged, her voice tight with urgency. "This night driver guy, Emory, he knows what happened. What about Cal's phone?"

The door swung open without warning. David stood framed in the doorway, his thin lips already forming words of accusation. "What about it? Do you know who he's been contacting a lot in the last 24—"

His words halted as his gaze swept the room. Lyric tracked his eyes, watched as they went for the list still displayed on Mira's screen.

Lyric shifted tactics instantaneously and drew his attention back to her. "Yes! I have a reporter coming in to cover the story about the death of—"

David stepped toward her, one hand raised as if to physically block her words. "Bup-bup-bup OK!! Mira here doesn't need to know everything—"

Mira, ever courteous, turned away from the confrontation. In doing so, she noticed the list still displayed on her screen. With a swift keystroke, she brought up a fresh browser tab, masking the incriminating evidence.

"Keep at it, Gerğes," Lyric instructed, using Mira's surname with deliberate formality.

Mira nodded, her expression exuding professional and diligent urgency. Lyric and David exited the room, tension crackling between them like static electricity.

Behind them, Mira rose from her chair and closed her office door, sealing herself away with the secrets they'd unearthed. She let out a soft huff of relief, grateful that David hadn't noticed the damning evidence on her screen.

***

Inside the Governor's office, David reclined against Rada's desk, his lanky frame draped across the mahogany edge with unearned comfort. A smug half-smile played across his thin lips, the expression of a man who believed himself the puppet master.

Lyric stood near the closed door, her spine pressed against the wall—cornered, yet still calculating. Her mind raced ahead, crafting lies she could deliver with enough conviction to pass as truth.

"I was thinking *The Journal*, but that's too friendly to us," she said, her voice measured despite her racing heart. "We need respectable: *The Washington Post*."

Rada lounged on her guest couch, reveling in Lyric's pitch of the kinds of political games she loved—the misdirection, the manipulation, the creation of narrative to serve her ends. David nodded along, watching Rada as much as he did Lyric.

"Made some calls," Lyric continued, the fabrication flowing smoothly. "A disinterested 3rd party will tip-off my friend at *The Post* that a fringe magazine writer down here is working this story 'from the terrorist's perspective.'"

"I fight terrorism," Rada replied, her face lighting up. "Love it. Go on."

Lyric maintained her composure, though revulsion churned in her stomach. How easily Rada seized any chance to climb in stature and image.

"My friend at *The Post* will come here to find out what the fringe guy has."

David pushed himself off the desk, his movement sharp and predatory. "The fringe <u>woman</u>, right? The liberal..."

His eyes narrowed as he searched Lyric's face for reaction. He was fishing, probing for a scapegoat they could cast in the role of villain.

Lyric and Rada exchanged glances, momentary confusion binding them. Lyric shook her head—a firm refusal to engage with his transparent attempt to build a specific cover narrative.

"Fine, what's the fringe writer have?" David pressed, annoyance creeping into his voice.

The corner of Rada's mouth twitched upward. She found amusement in David's failure to grasp the subtlety of the ruse. There was no "fringe guy"—the phantom writer existed solely as bait to lure legitimate press attention.

"Whatever we say, David," Rada answered in mocking tones, exasperation coloring her tone. "Lyric, go on—"

"I don't want too many people knowing—" David interrupted, his voice rising.

"There's no 'loose ends' here, David!" Rada snapped.

She rolled her eyes toward Lyric, inviting her to share in her disdain. David caught the exchange, his jaw tightening as he recognized himself as the object of their derision.

"As long as the front gate lets my *Post* reporter on campus, we're good," Lyric continued smoothly, redirecting the conversation. "And you come out of this the hero."

"I like it. Perfect. You are good," Rada purred, approval radiating from her expression.

A sharp knock interrupted their scheming, three decisive raps against the wooden door.

"Come in!" Rada called.

In one fluid motion, Lyric slipped behind the opening door, pressing herself into the shadow where she could remain invisible to whoever entered. The door swung inward, revealing the large State Trooper Captain. His posture rigid as steel, he stood at the threshold, directing his attention to David.

"You wanted to see me?" The Captain's voice carried the flat, professional tone of a man accustomed to following orders without question.

"A reporter from *The Post* will be arriving on campus," Rada informed him, voice shifting seamlessly into her official register. "Tell the Trooper at the entrance to let him in."

From her hidden position, Lyric peered through the crack where door met jamb. Beyond the Captain, she spotted a nervous-looking Bookstore Clerk shifting from foot to foot in the hallway. Another witness to Lyric and Cal's date last night.

"Maybe it's time to bring this witness up to see the telemarketers upstairs?" David suggested, the casual tone of his voice at odds with the intensity in his eyes.

Rada knew where David was steering the witness – to trigger the next phase of their campaign; "Finding" the body.

The Captain held out his hand. "I'll need the master key."

David extracted a plastic card from his sport coat and crossed the room to deliver it. As he reached the doorway, he turned the Captain away from Rada, leaning close to murmur words not meant for the Governor's ears.

"Send one of your men with him," David whispered, his voice reaching Lyric only because of her proximity. "I called you for a travel project, off-campus. Gimme one minute."

From her position, Lyric observed Rada pinch the bridge of her nose, disgust evident in the gesture. The implication struck Lyric with cold clarity—this "travel project" meant Emory, the driver who knew too much. David was arranging his elimination.

Rada's office door closed with a soft click, sealing them once more in the artificial safety of the office.

"Any news on the elevator video?" Rada asked, tension threading through her voice.

Lyric stepped away from the wall, mind racing to formulate a response which would buy her time. "A little snafu with the elevators... Luckily, it's backed up in the cloud."

"What?" Rada jerked upright in her chair.

"How?" David demanded, alarm flashing across his face.

"I'll go see what the quality's like," Lyric replied with practiced nonchalance.

She planted the seed of paranoia and watched it take root in their expressions. Let them chew on that possibility while she continued her race to save Emory and herself. Without another word, she exited the office, allowing the door to close behind her.

Just outside Rada's door, the Captain stood alone, waiting for his special assignment orders from David like a loyal hound.

"Miss," he began as she passed. "A witness from Bingo's—"

"—Bookstore just went upstairs, yup," Lyric completed the sentence, never breaking stride.

She hurried toward Mira's office, but a thought stopped her mid-step. The lie she had told needed buttressing. She veered toward Estelle's scheduling office, mind already constructing the right blend of technical jargon and confident delivery.

Estelle glanced up from her computer screen, surprise registering on her soft face as Lyric appeared in the doorway.

"Good news," Lyric announced, keeping her voice low and conspiratorial. "Just found out there might be cloud backup of the elevator cam. If anybody asks, I'm downloading TCP packets from a virtual server cache."

Estelle blinked, clearly buffaloed by the technical terminology washing over her. Lyric noted the confusion with satisfaction—incomprehensible jargon often proved more convincing than plausible lies.

"Yep. It's very complicated. And underway. If anybody asks..."

Estelle shrugged her acceptance of the ruse, and Lyric ducked back into the bullpen, mission accomplished.

She pushed open the door to Mira's office without knocking. Inside, Mira sat hunched over her desk, phone pressed to her ear, on hold. The room hummed with tension and the quiet electronic buzz of equipment.

"Did you get an email with Cal's unlocked phone data or something?" Lyric demanded, her patience evaporating instantly.

Mira shook her head. "I didn't see it."

"Look!" Lyric's frustration mounted, each second of inaction a luxury they could not afford.

Mira clicked through her emails, her eyes scanning the screen with growing urgency. "Yeah. Shit. Missed this."

"Mother fuc—" Lyric bit off the curse. "David's CC'd?"

Mira nodded confirmation, her expression grim.

"Shit. Keep calling," Lyric instructed, hands clenching and unclenching at her sides. "But you gotta search his stuff. Print anything good."

"Whaddya mean good?" Mira asked, confusion clouding her features.

"The affair, blackmail…" Lyric's voice cracked with strain. Lyric needed Mira to engage her mind and create solutions. "Please!"

Lyric stormed from the room, leaving Mira bruised. Mira took a deep breath and doubled her focus back onto the list of island houses.

***

The metal door of the stairwell banged open as Lyric burst into the shaded back parking lot that sloped down beside the buildings. She sprinted down the path, her footfalls echoing off the brick.

Her gaze darted across the landscape, searching for surveillance, for pursuit. Every window became a potential observer, every corner a possible ambush. She raced toward the back doors to the stores in the next building. The building where Cal's Pilates studio was, where he'd once moved with grace and confidence.

The first back door loomed ahead, its back door a possible sanctuary or a risk. Lyric threw the door open and slipped inside, pulling it shut behind her. A sticker on the door revealed that Lyric's play was to consult the mall's travel agency…

Lyric moved swiftly through the corridor lined with posters of exotic beaches and snow-capped mountains on the walls, promising escape to the lucky few.

Lyric emerged from the back hallway into the main space of the storefront office, she approached the row of desks from behind.

She slid into the nearest chair, positioning herself with her back to the entrance. A young agent looked up from her computer screen, surprise flickering across her face at Lyric's breathless arrival from the rear.

"Hi. I'm interested in ah...island?" Lyric offered, forcing a charming smile. She needed an ally and self-deprecating humor always disarmed people.

The agent laughed, a sound so normal it seemed out of place in Lyric's unraveling world. "What island do you have in mind?"

"Not Hilton Head," Lyric replied aloud but to herself. She kept the charm offensive on: "Dunno yet, exactly. Um, it's basically impossible to fly anywhere without showing ID, right?"

Her eyes darted toward the front door, scanning for police walking witnesses door-to-door. The glass storefront offered no protection, only transparency.

"Did a woman in Yoga pants—with a few State Police come through here?" she asked, managing to keep the urgency from her voice.

The agent frowned, confusion replacing her professional smile. "No. What _is_ going on, do you know?"

The witness and Police hadn't arrived yet—she had minutes, perhaps seconds, before this temporary haven became another trap. Her gaze flicked repeatedly toward the entrance, anticipating the moment when uniforms would darken the doorway.

"I don't know what's going on," she lied. "Can I borrow this? Can I use your bathroom?"

She snatched a pen from the desk and rose in one fluid motion, already moving toward the rear of the office.

"Sure. On the right," the agent called after her, bewildered.

Lyric disappeared into the shadowed hallway. The sound of a printer's paper tray opening and closing drifted back to the main office, a curious interruption that caught the ear of the travel agent.

The bathroom door closed with a soft click as Lyric twisted the lock. She leaned against the wall, heart hammering against her ribs. From her pocket, she extracted her phone, pulling up the photo of the island list. Her hand trembled as she pressed the borrowed pen to purloined paper, copying the information with haste.

A splash of color caught her eye. Between two framed travel posters—one of a Caribbean sunset, another of Mediterranean cliffs—hung an advertisement for "Chartered Yachts." The image showed a gleaming speedboat at rest in crystalline waters, models diving from its deck into the perfect blue below.

Revelation struck her like lightning. No ID checks. No passenger manifests. No questions asked…for the right price.

Lyric burst from the bathroom, renewed by purpose. The travel agent stood as she approached.

"I have to run," Lyric announced, handing over the paper with her handwritten notes. "But these islands…"

She tapped the page with a fingernail.

"How long would it take you to get a chartered boat on standby from each of these islands? To Washington DC. One passenger. Let me know when it's ready and I'll tell you which one."

From her envelope labeled "Lyric," she extracted her per-diem cash—now repurposed as a down-payment of sorts. The agent's eyes widened at the sight of the money. Lyric reclaimed the paper, bending to scribble her number on it.

"My number. If you get this done fast, I'll pay a premium, in cash."

Behind her, through the plate glass window, movement caught her eye. State Police officers converged on the travel agency, the Pilates student witness in tow.

"I'm Leyla Ger-shh…"

She extended her hand for a farewell shake, but the agent's gaze had shifted, focusing on something beyond Lyric's shoulder. Lyric could guess what it was. The agent's widening eyes told Lyric everything she needed to know.

"Shh…it. I'll be back."

Before the agent could respond, Lyric had slipped past her, a ghost evaporating into the air. The backdoor slammed shut.

The parking lot welcomed her return with indifference. Lyric ran up the path, retracing her earlier route. The Stand Strong PAC's back stairway doors beckoned, promising a return to the heart of the conspiracy—a place of danger, yes, but also of answers to some of her many lingering worries.

The main bullpen was again silent as Lyric headed for Mira's office. The Anxious State Trooper marched toward her with purpose, suspicion etched into every line of his face. His eyes bored into hers, seeking guilt, seeking confirmation of his theory—that she was guilty of something.

"Wait," the trooper demanded. "Evening shift at the restaurants is starting up. If any waitresses served Cal and Chan, we'll have more witnesses. Very soon."

"That's…just great." Lyric kept her voice steady, though her skin burned with apprehension. Each second prolonged this confrontation increased her danger.

The trooper's gaze never left her face, searching for any flicker of guilt, any sign of weakness he could exploit.

"The suspect is in a Pilates class," she offered, inspiration striking. "Assume it'll be healthy food. So leave the booze and burgers for last. Go spread the word."

His eyes narrowed. "David wanted to see me."

"...You have your orders."

The words carried more authority than she had any right to claim. For a moment, their eyes locked in silent combat. Then he turned away, defeated but not convinced, his departure marked by the rigid set of his shoulders.

Lyric watched him go, her momentary victory hollow. In his hands, her clever diversion might collapse like a house of cards. Time was running out. She momentarily forgot was she needed to do next, and then remembered: Mira.

A BREAK

When Lyric burst through the door Mira was standing, her phone pressed to her ear, face alight with excitement.

"...actually if you could hold for one minute, a Director of the Governor's campaign would like to double check. Can you hold?" Mira's voice carried a newfound authority. She pressed her finger against the phone's screen, muting the call, and turned to Lyric with triumphant eyes. "Bermuda. Emory arrived, there's a security guy and a housekeeper."

"Holy shit, thank God." Relief washed over Lyric's face, her shoulders dropping a fraction. "Good job. Map."

Lyric seized the phone from Mira's outstretched hand. Meanwhile, Mira's fingers flew across her keyboard, pulling up a website displaying a detailed map of Bermuda. She zoomed in on a specific location marked with a red pin, the image growing larger with each click. Lyric leaned forward, hunger in her gaze as she studied the screen.

"Hi, is this Emory?" she spoke into the phone, her voice controlled despite the urgency pulsing through her.

She pointed at Mira's computer screen, directing the younger woman's actions. "Satellite view. Zoom in." The map transformed, revealing rooftops, swimming pools, and winding roads. "Nice pool."

Returning her attention to the phone call, Lyric continued, "Look out to the backyard—down at the water's edge, is that a dock?" Mira watched as Lyric listened. "There's a rowboat? Perfect."

She activated the speakerphone function and appropriated Mira's computer mouse, taking control. "I'm getting you outta there. Gotta zoom out a bit and print this—"

The door swung open without warning—David slipped in, weasel-like, his narrow face intent. "Your *Post* reporter is on campus."

Mira's fingers danced across the keyboard, changing tabs to conceal the Bermuda map. David's eyes flicked toward the screen, but he arrived a heartbeat too late to glimpse what she'd hidden.

"Can you have him call me direct?" Lyric asked Mira, maintaining her composure despite the intrusion.

"No, his phone doesn't work...there." Mira's voice wavered slightly.

"Y'all talkin' to me?" Emory's voice blared from the phone speaker.

Lyric shot Mira a warning glare—hard eyes boring into her. Mira scrambled to disable the speaker function, her fingertip jabbing at the screen.

"Who's that-?" David's brows furrowed.

"Mira, print," Lyric commanded to interrupt him, rising from her chair in one fluid movement.

She exited the room, grabbing David's arm and pulling him along. The lie flowed from her lips with practiced ease: "That's the technician. The elevator video servers are in a basement, he'll call me when he's above ground. C'mon..."

The main bullpen stretched before them, a sea of empty desks caught in the afternoon light. Lyric guided David toward Rada's office, giving him a slight shove.

"I'll be right with our media—Go prep the Governor for camera." Her command sliced through the air.

David resisted her push but turned on her fast. His fingers wrapped around her wrist, unexpected and tight. "Whoa. I don't what you think you—"

"Let go." Two words, sharp as flint.

Lyric twisted her arm free from his grasp. She jogged across the vacant bullpen, her vision blurring as unwanted tears welled up. Rage and fear braided together inside her chest, a constricting rope she could barely breathe around.

***

Outside, the afternoon sun beat down on the main building's front facade. Lyric burst through the front doors, her breath coming in quick gasps. She ran across the sidewalk to the road.

From across the village green a distant observer migh[t] have seen Lyric striding purposefully, head bowed toward a hybrid hatchback parked along the curb. Sh[e] dropped to one knee beside the vehicle, peering throug[h] the open window.

Inside the aged car, which smelled of fast food and ai[r] freshener, sat a bearded, graying man. His tubby fram[e] filled the driver's seat, hands resting on the steerin[g] wheel. Beside him, a young woman barely out of he[r] teens fidgeted nervously.

"You're the fixer Tae-sung Lee sent?" Lyric's voice carried equal parts hope and skepticism.

The man nodded, his eyes shrewd beneath bushy brows. "Yeah. You're Lyric. I'm Duke."

"This is your Assistant? I was told it was a guy! Shit." Frustration sharpened her tone. She addressed the driver again. "Drive around to the back lot. Park outside the door to the Travel Agency. I'll be there soon."

Her attention snapped to the young woman. "You, look older and come with me."

Lyric pivoted and sprinted toward the entrance, the Assistant scrambling from Duke's car, clutching a bag as she hurried to keep pace. The hybrid pulled away from the curb, its electric motor humming softly as it circled toward the rear parking area.

As the car departed, it revealed a figure across the village green—outside the Always 21 Boutique, the Funky Cashier stood, inhaling deeply from a vape pen during her break. A cloud of chemicals enveloped her face as she squinted, focusing on Lyric's distant form. Recognition dawned in her eyes, followed by apprehension. She glanced around nervously, searching for any sign of a State Cop, her fingers tightening around the vape pen.

The ground floor elevator lobby of the main building sat silent as Lyric stood beside the Fixer's Assistant, studying the illuminated number panel above the elevator doors. The number "3" glowed steady, refusing to change. Their whispers barely disturbed the silence of the space.

"Tae-sung Lee wired us this. For you." The Assistant's voice carried the slight tremor of inexperience. She reached into her bag and extracted an envelope, passing it to Lyric with furtive movements.

Lyric opened the unsealed envelope. Inside lay a thick stack of crisp hundred-dollar bills. She rifled through them swiftly, her expression unreadable.

"Okay. Here's what we're going to do." Lyric tucked the envelope into her pocket, her movements economical. "You're gonna pretend to be a reporter for *The Washington Post*. All you do is put your phone on the desk and say you're recording the conversation."

The Assistant's eyes widened. "Do I? Um..." She paused, noticing Lyric's attention had drifted upward. "What's wrong?"

Lyric frowned at the elevator display where the light had halted on "2," an unexpected detour. "Someone's come from 3." She exhaled sharply, unease crossing her features.

"Sure, why not." Lyric answered the Assistant. Impatient intensity radiating from her. "Listen, say this: 'I want to hear your side of the story.' OK? If they ask you anything, you only answer: 'I am protecting my sources.' Don't ask any questions. Don't interrupt them. Only say 'go on.' A lot. Got a notebook?"

The elevator announced its arrival with a cheerful ding. The Assistant nodded, her face a mask of concentration. The doors slid open, revealing an empty car.

Inside the elevator, the artificial light cast harsh shadows across Lyric's face as she continued her rapid-fire instructions. "Write down random words pulled from what they say. Occasionally cross out a word. It's infuriating." Her lips curved into a mirthless smile. "Remember, they'll blabber to hold their audience's attention because politics is theater for ugly people. So don't give them anything."

Another ding heralded their arrival. The doors parted, revealing the third floor. Lyric raised her finger to her lips, silencing the Assistant as they stepped out.

The main bullpen sprawled before them, empty desks and partitions. Lyric fast-walked, the Assistant hurrying to match her pace. They passed the thin, anxious State Trooper whose eyes bored into them, trailing them across the room. Lyric acknowledged him with a terse nod, her stride never faltering.

Moments later, they arrived Rada's door. Lyric rapped sharply against the wood.

"Come in!" David's voice called from within.

Lyric pushed the door open and entered alone, closing it swiftly behind her.

Inside, before Lyric could launch into her prepared speech, David spoke:

"We have another witness. A cashier at the Always 21 clothing store. Chan Power entered the building."

Lyric pivoted smoothly, deflecting this newest problem without missing a beat. "Fantastic. The reporter is perfect. Here's why: she's green. She'll print whatever you say, verbatim. Like Maggie Haberman stenography. Ready?"

Rada perked up at this assessment, anticipation lighting her eyes. Lyric opened the door with a flourish. "Come on in."

The young Assistant stepped inside, her posture straightening as she assumed her role. Lyric gestured toward her, improvising. "This is...Layla George. Our Campaign Manager David, and here is Governor Rada Waylos. Layla is all ears."

Lyric nodded at the Assistant, winked conspiratorially at David, and ducked out of the office.

Lyric made it three steps into the bullpen before David followed her, pulling Rada's office door closed behind him.

"What are you doing? Get in there—" Lyric hissed, stopping short.

"I had a feeling..." David's voice dropped to a confidential murmur. He paused, noting Lyric's confused expression. "Pin it on the liberal. It's good. I what you're doing."

"<u>Not</u> what we're doing." Lyric's voice carried steel beneath its surface. "I'm doing what the Governor asked; A big splashy media play—I suggest you get on board. Cut the shit. Go!"

David's face hardened into a mask of suspicion, but he stalked back inside Rada's office without further argument. The moment the door clicked shut, Lyric darted across the bullpen to David's office.

She slipped inside and closed the door with barely a whisper of sound. Racing behind David's desk, her eyes locked onto a prize—the plaid shopping bag tucked underneath now bulged with her canvas tote and green jacket. She snatched it up, triumph flashing across her face.

"Lyric."

The voice froze her in place. She snapped upright to find Estelle peering through the doorway, her expression sphinxlike, unreadable. The older woman's eyes took in the scene—Lyric behind David's desk, the plaid bag clutched in her hands.

"Little question for you..." Estelle's voice carried a deceptive lightness. Estelle nodded back toward the bullpen, a clear summons for Lyric to follow her outside.

Sunlight filtered through a dingy narrow window set in the walls of the faux-clock tower staircase. The two women descended several flights, their footsteps echoing in the hollow chamber. Estelle moved with surprising agility for her age, while Lyric followed, hyperaware of every sound around them.

At the bottom landing, a heavy steel door stood partially ajar. Estelle pushed it open without hesitation, revealing the building's cellar beyond.

They entered the underground space, crossing a rough cement floor rarely touched. A chain-link fence partition bisected the cellar, and beyond it sat a security camera station. Monitors glowed blue in the dim light, but the chair before the screens remained conspicuously empty.

"I called the man who *should* be here," Estelle said, her voice soft yet penetrating in the confined space. "He said David cut and pasted the video to an orange hard drive. As in 'delete.' Then David sent this security man home. The man also told me there's no TCP packet cloud anything. So you're both lying. Why?"

The sweet timbre of Estelle's voice carried sharp disappointment which struck Lyric with unexpected force. Lyric's iron facade cracked, revealing vulnerability beneath.

"No!" Lyric's voice broke. "David's lying because he's dangerous. I'm lying because I think I know what..." She paused, struggling to voice her suspicion. "...happened to Caleb."

Estelle studied Lyric's face, noting the raw pain in her eyes. The older woman's expression softened as she recalled her own misgivings.

"I believe you..." Estelle moved closer, her voice dropping to a whisper. "Why did David hide that boy's phone in his safe?"

Lyric dropped the rectangular plaid bag, her shock palpable. "But the cop—"

"Only had his laptop." Estelle's eyes shone with determination. "I want to help."

Lyric absorbed this crucial information, processing its implications. A slow smile spread across her face as she recognized she'd gained an ally in this most unlikely of places.

A moment later, Lyric peered cautiously through the cellar door before stepping out onto the metal stairs leading up the airy stairwell of the clock tower. Sunlight slashed through the space once more, a stark contrast to the cellar's gloom. One flight above, several State Troopers climbed toward the PAC office, their movements hurried and purposeful.

Lyric prepared to race after them when Estelle's hand closed around her arm. The older woman nodded toward the cellar and winked conspiratorially. "Our secret."

Lyric squeezed Estelle's hand in silent gratitude before bolting up the stairs. She maneuvered around the troopers, positioning herself ahead of the lead officer—a young man whose face shone with excitement.

"Body's been found," he announced, breathless.

"Wait." Lyric raised her hand to halt his progress. "A reporter's in the office. Can't let on something's up. I'll make sure the coast is clear."

She prevented him from entering the rear door to the office suite, slipping inside by herself and closing the door firmly behind her.

The main bullpen stretched before her. Lyric sprinted toward the printer stationed against the far wall. She snatched several pages from its output tray, one prominently displaying a map of Bermuda. Ignoring the troopers waiting in the stairwell, she dashed across the open floor toward the elevator bank.

Seconds later, sweat beaded on her forehead as she watched the illuminated numbers above the elevator. The car descended from the third floor—where the campaign's residences were located. Pressing her ear against the narrow gap between the elevator doors, Lyric caught muffled male voices from inside. Another complication. Another threat.

She pivoted, racing toward the campaign office bullpen. As the elevator doors announced their opening with a cheerful ding, Lyric ducked into an empty desk alcove. She dropped to the floor, crawling beneath the desk. Her muscles burned from exertion as she tucked herself against a cubicle wall stanchion. The wool cap overheated her, and she yanked it off.

Her phone vibrated. "Duncan Travel" flashed on the screen. She silenced it immediately.

From her hidden vantage point, Lyric could see only legs as the State Cops hurried past, accompanied by a distraught young man she recognized as the Bookstore Clerk Witness. Their footsteps faded as they moved deeper into the office toward Rada and David's doors.

Seizing her opportunity, Lyric bolted for the elevators. As the doors began sliding closed, she slipped inside and pressed herself against the wall.

The elevator descended in silence. Lyric drew one deep breath, centering herself in the corner. When the doors parted on the ground floor, two more State Troopers entered—accompanied by the Funky Cashier from Always-21.

Lyric lunged toward the opening, desperate to escape. She collided with a third trooper trailing behind the others. Their bodies connected with enough force to rock him backward. Lyric wrenched herself free, but his voice followed her:

"Ma'am! The witness—"

She kept moving toward the lobby's rear exit, her face angled away from the Funky Cashier. "Go wait on the office stairs!" she commanded without turning.

Lyric pushed through the back door, disappearing out of the lobby. Inside the elevator, the Funky Cashier craned her neck, staring after Lyric's retreating form.

"Who was that?" the cashier asked, her voice tinged with suspicious recognition. Her eyes narrowed, an ominous glare hardening.

***

Lyric dashed down the sidewalk in the rear of the main building. Her footsteps pounded against the concrete. The wind whipped through her hair.

She reached the parked hybrid hatchback with a thud, yanking open the door. Duke the Fixer sat inside, eyes wide with expectation.

"One more minute!" Lyric shouted, her voice raw with urgency.

Without waiting for a response, she spun away, running toward the back door of the Travel Agency. Her heart hammered against her ribs.

Inside the Travel Agency, Lyric collapsed into the chair across from the unsuspecting Travel Agent's desk—the same agent she had tasked with research earlier. Sweat beaded on her forehead, her chest rising and falling with each labored breath.

"Bermuda. It's Bermuda, here," she declared, her voice steadier than her hands.

Lyric handed over the folded printout Mira had created—a map view and coordinates of the private dock at Emory's hiding place in Bermuda.

"Can I borrow a hair-tie?" Lyric quickly said as an aside, and as the Agent opened her desk drawer to offer a small elastic, Lyric continued quickly: "Right there. The chartered boat - has to pick up my passenger - here."

She handed over a thick envelope of cash and then put her hair up in a ponytail. The Travel Agent's eyes widened slightly when she eyed the 100 dollar bills.

"He has a rowboat. He can paddle out, or whatever - if it's too shallow. Leaving now. Are we good?"

The Travel Agent counted the hundred-dollar bills with practiced efficiency, her fingers dancing across the paper. She glanced up, a smile spreading across her face—worth more than any verbal confirmation.

In David's office, shadows stretched across his desk as paced with theatrical gravity. The space had grown claustrophobic with the addition of a State Cop and the Bookstore Clerk Witness, whose quiet sobs punctuated the tense silence.

David's voice dropped, conveying false solemnity.

"Caleb - dead? I need a minute."

He rubbed his face, a pantomime of grief. Before he could continue the charade, a sharp knock rattled his door. The State Cop opened it, revealing another State Cop standing there with the Funky Cashier.

The Statie cleared his throat, his voice tight. "Chan Power was just seen..."

Behind them, the Blue Ridge Distillery's glum waiter also peered into the room, his posture slouched beside the Anxious Statie. The air vibrated with tension—so many witnesses in such a tight space, surely a powder keg awaiting a spark.

Meanwhile, in the parked hybrid hatchback, the Fixer held a mini audio recorder in front of Lyric.

"Hold on hold on, who was murdered?" Duke, the Fixer asked, eyebrows knitting together.

"Her lover," Lyric replied, her voice flat.

The Fixer stared at Lyric, skepticism etched into every line of his face.

"They're looking for a scapegoat, call your assistant, get her out of there," Lyric urged, panic edging into her voice.

"Come on, Rada's a moderate." The Fixer's voice carried a note of disbelief.

Lyric responded with a sideways glance, her expression screaming: *bitch, please*. Her eyes held the weariness of someone who had witnessed the evil truth behind Rada's façade.

In Rada's large office suite, David rushed in, closing the door behind him with unnecessary force. The sound reverberated through the room, a small exclamation point to his entrance.

"...Sorry for the interruption," he offered, smoothing his tie with one hand.

The Assistant's phone buzzed—evidently not for the first time. Rada glanced toward it, annoyance flickering across her face.

"Very popular. Go ahead..." Rada waved a hand, permission granted.

"Sorry," the Assistant murmured, reaching for her phone.

She checked her text messages, eyes widening slightly at what she read:

Get out of there now.

"I need to be going." The Assistant rose from her chair, gathering her belongings with forced casualness.

"Wait. I've got something for you in my office. One minute." David's words sliced through the air, commanding rather than requesting.

He exited Rada's office quickly, crossing the bullpen where the full collection of witnesses had gathered—the Bookstore Clerk, the Pilates Student, the Funky Cashier, and the Brewhouse Glum Waiter. Their presence created a strange tableau, like a jury assembled to pass judgment.

David rushed into his office, darting behind his desk. His eyes searched then slammed shut. The blood drained from his face as realization dawned: the Plaid Shopping Bag was gone. His evidence, his leverage, had vanished.

Back in the bullpen, the Assistant opened Rada's door to leave. "I have to go..."

As she stepped into the open space, revealing herself fully to the assembled witnesses, the Funky Cashier lunged forward, finger pointing accusingly.

"HER! SHE came in with the killer!"

The Anxious Statie's voice rose above the sudden commotion. "Lyric! That'd be Lyric. Find Lyric!"

David stood frozen, unable to intervene as the State Troopers sprang into action around him. His carefully constructed entrapment ideas began to collapse. David's expression dropped to consternation in the space of a heartbeat—he watched his plan disintegrate before his eyes.

***

Glass doors burst open as State Cops rushed out from the ground floor lobby. Their boots thundered across the concrete, echoing in the autumn air. They split into groups, moving with military precision—predators seeking prey. One particular officer charged down the pathway between buildings toward the back parking lot, his face set in grim determination.

In the parked hybrid hatchback, the Fixer's weathered hands gripped his audio recorder before Lyric. His eyes widened as he spotted the approaching officer through the windshield. Panic surged across his deeply carved features. Beside him, Lyric twisted in the passenger seat, scrambling toward the door with frantic movements.

"I have to stay and save this guy's life." Then she reminded Duke, "You work for *The Post*. Go!" Her voice cracked with urgency.

Without waiting for a response, she flung herself from the vehicle and bolted toward the travel agency's rear entrance, her figure blurring with speed.

The hybrid hatchback's engine whined in protest as the Fixer accelerated away, hybrid mother straining a mechanical cry of distress.

Inside the travel agency's back hallway, Lyric dashed inside, slamming the door behind her and bolting the door. The lock engaged with a satisfying thud.

She continued through the office, her breathing ragged, her footsteps squeaking on the polished cement floor. She skidded to a halt at the desk, grabbing the printout she had left with the Travel Agent.

"Just need a number off this..." she muttered, her fingers trembling as she punched a series of digits into her cell phone—the number for the Bermuda house where Emory had been shipped.

A loud banging erupted from the back door, the metal frame shuddering with each impact. The Travel Agent's head snapped up, eyes wide with alarm. She rose from her chair, moving toward the commotion. Lyric seized the opportunity, darting through the front door and into the blinding sunlight beyond.

The front sidewalk stretched before her, exposed and vulnerable. Lyric ran for the walkway between buildings. She darted inside the narrow passage, only to freeze mid-stride. At the opposite end, the State Cop had evidently given up trying to get inside the back door and had started for the front. He turned into the walkway and began to run toward her with purposeful strides.

She spun around, doubling back with the desperate energy of cornered prey. When she again reached the front side walk, her gaze flicked upward toward the main lobby door where more officers emerged, jogging down the sidewalk in their heavy boots. The rhythmic thud of their footfalls measured out her dwindling options.

The Pilates studio stood farther down the path. Lyric sprinted toward it as fast as her feet could carry her. She burst through the front door, disrupting the serene atmosphere within.

A yoga class froze in various poses of contortion—a tableau of surprised faces and balanced limbs. Yelps of protest squealing from the yogis as Lyric careened through their midst, disturbing their carefully maintained equilibrium. She paid them no mind, focused solely on reaching the exit at the rear of the studio.

The cool air outside the studio caressed her flushed skin as she emerged. The coast momentarily clear, she raced toward the main building's clock tower back door. Her phone finally connected a call as she ran, the electronic ring cutting through her labored breathing.

"Emory? ...It's me. Can you email me? I need what time you brought Rada to the office and then back to her house—" Her words tumbled over one another, urgent and breathless.

The clock tower loomed above her. She slipped inside the stairwell's back door, the heavy metal door closing behind her with a resonant clang.

Within the clock tower stairwell, steel steps spiraled upward. Lyric placed one foot on the first step, her body poised for ascent.

She froze, horror washing over her face as she listened to the voice on the other end of the line.

"Hold on...No. Whaddya mean you didn't bring her to her house? Nononono..." Her voice cracked, disbelief and desperation intertwining.

Her breath came out in shudders. Whatever Emory had said had obliterated her plan, leaving her stranded in this empty tower with nowhere left to run. Inexorable, the approach of consequences found her no longer able to evade.

TRAPPED

Blue siren lights sliced through the afternoon air as the gray State Police cruiser raced from the front entrance along the driveway. The vehicle accelerated in a powerful hum toward the main office building's front lobby near the faux clock tower.

Duke the Fixer—an older man with weathered skin and eyes of hard-lived experience—sat inside his hybrid hatchback at the loading zone in front of the elevator lobby. Hearing the turbo-charged engine of the Police truck approach, his knuckles whitened around the steering wheel. The police cruiser skidded to an abrupt halt, positioning itself to block Duke's car. The screech of tires echoed across the village green.

A State Trooper emerged from the cruiser in one fluid motion. Sunlight glinted off his aviator sunglasses as he drew his weapon, aiming it steadily at the hybrid.

"Get out of the car!" he commanded, his voice carrying across the distance between them.

Without lowering his weapon, the Trooper pressed a button on his shoulder radio. The small device crackled to life.

"I got 'em trying to leave," he reported, his eyes never leaving the hybrid.

The Fixer complied, pushing open his little car door with deliberate slowness. He stepped out with hands raised above his head, palms open, face impassive despite the gun trained on his chest.

***

Inside Mira's spacious office, tension hung thick in the air. David stood behind her chair. Sweat beaded along his receding hairline as he hovered over Mira, who sat rigid with fear. Her eyes darted between her phone—which displayed "LYRIC CALLING" on its screen—and David's looming presence.

"Find out where she's hiding," David snapped, impatience radiating from every pore.

Mira hesitated, her fingers hovering over the phone. The continued ringing sliced through the silence of the room. David's patience broke. He shoved her shoulder, hard enough to make her flinch with shock. The message was clear.

Mira pressed the answer button, bringing the phone to her ear.

"Hello?" Her voice wavered despite her efforts to control it.

David snatched the phone from her grasp, his movements swift and aggressive. He tapped the speaker button, filling the room with the crackling sound of the connection.

"—to print something for me..." Lyric's voice came through, then paused. "Take me off speaker. Mira?"

Mira leaned toward the phone, her eyes locked on David's face. "David is here, asking where you are."

David's expression darkened, rage flashing across his features at Mira's betrayal. Mira stared back at him, a small act of defiance in a moment where she held little power.

In the clock tower stairwell of the main building, Lyric pressed her phone closer to her ear, listening intently. Her mind raced, processing the information in Mira's careful words. Something wasn't right.

"I snuck away. I'm in a cab," she lied, her voice steady despite the panic rising in her chest.

She ended the call and tucked the phone into her pocket, her breathing shallow. The stairwell stretched above her, concrete steps winding upward into shadow. She continued climbing, each step placed with care to minimize noise.

A few flights below, the distinctive crash of the back door opening froze her in place. Voices echoed up the stairwell, bouncing off concrete walls. Lyric moved to the edge of the stairs, carefully peering downward.

At the bottom of the stairwell, several State Troopers escorted The Fixer across the landing. Their boots scuffed against the concrete floor as they directed him toward a set of metal steps leading down to the cellar. The steel door closed behind them with a resounding clang which reverberated through the entire stairwell.

Mira's office door swung open without warning. A bald State Trooper stepped inside, his gaze sweeping the room before settling on David.

"Sir. The accomplice is in custody downstairs. We found this." The Trooper lifted the plaid shopping bag—the same one Lyric had hidden earlier.

As soon as they exited, Mira grabbed her phone, fingers flying across the screen as she sped off a text message:

They found a bag. ???

Her phone rang immediately—LYRIC CALLING displayed on the screen. Mira answered without hesitation.

Lyric stood outside the Governor's Office's back door, her heart hammering as she whispered into the phone.

"Did you print the proof I sent you?"

Lyric could only hope for the best.

Meanwhile, David closed his office door with a soft click. Alone at last. His face transformed to reveal something cold and calculating underneath. He reached into the plaid shopping bag with deliberate precision.

He extracted both the canvas bag and green coat—and inspected them carefully. He could manage to salvage his plan. He would pin everything on this *Post* reporter. He would keep Lyric in his inner circle. His breath came out in a relieved exhale.

The punch key lock of his office safe beeped a few times before the mechanism surrendered with a metallic groan. From within its depths, David retrieved Rada's pistol, weighing it in his palm. The cold steel felt heavy. His hand dipped back into the safe, emerging with Cal's phone. David studied the device for several heartbeats before returning it to its resting place among his safe's secrets.

He tucked the gun into the waistband of his pants, the cold metal biting into the small of his back. Its presence altered his posture, straightened his spine.

Governor Rada's office suite was tense as the Fixer's Assistant stood, absolutely unwilling to sit as Rada and the bald State Police officer inside kept insisting she do.

David pushed through the door which bumped into Police officer standing guard. David approached the Assistant extending the plaid shopping bag toward her. Anxiety lined her face. Since Duke's message to "get out of there," she had been trying.

The officer's continued warnings that a situation was developing outside and that it would be unsafe if anyone left had worn thin. The Governor's anecdotes had chipped away at her patience, leaving nothing but raw nerves and irritation.

"Can I go now??" she asked, words clipped and sharp.

"I thought I'd lost this. For you. Yes you can go." David replied, his response cut short by a voice outside--

The office door remained ajar, a corner of the bullpen visible beyond; Mira appeared in this opening, her arm extended, her phone clutched desperately.

"Governor! You need to take this!" Urgency sculpted her words into something both brittle and commanding.

Just on the other side of the Governor's office wall, halfway up the clock tower, on the mid-flight landing

Lyric pressed her phone close, voice dropping to a whisper.

"Just hand your phone to Rada."

Without warning, the back door to the Stand Strong PAC offices exploded open into the clock tower. David froze in the doorway, muscles locking as his eyes found Lyric standing mere feet away. His hand dug into the Assistant's upper arm—the same vicious grip he had once used on Lyric herself.

Time crystallized around them. Fear pulsed between them, an electric current neither could break. Lyric's gaze dropped to the plaid bag dangling from David's other hand.

From somewhere in the bullpen beyond, a voice cut through the tense silence. The glum waiter from the Brewhouse pointed, recognition flashing across his face.

"There she is! That's her!"

The State Police officer guarding the witnesses raised his radio to his lips, voice resonating through the stairwell.

"10-20! Owl's Nest!"

Lyric spun on her heel, lunging down the stairs. Her footfalls echoed against steel and concrete, a percussion of panic and flight.

David turned back toward the officer, voice sharp as broken glass. "Stay with the Governor!"

On the ground floor of the clock tower, a State Police officer emerged from the cellar doorway, his radio crackling with static and urgent codes.

"Coming! 10-4!" His voice bounced off the industrial walls, multiplying into a chorus of danger.

His boots struck the steps with heavy thuds as he ascended to intercept Lyric.

A few flights up from him, Lyric peered over the railing and spotted the officer's steady climb. With no choice, she changed direction, legs burning as she pushed herself back upward instead of down, climbing past David, up toward the tower's hollow peak.

Outside, the main building's clock tower rose against the autumn sky, its fake stonework catching the late afternoon sun. State Police vehicles converged on the scene, tires screeching against asphalt as they pulled to abrupt stops before the main office.

Midway up the tower's height, a small window offered a glimpse of movement—Lyric's silhouette flashed past, a dark blur against the facade.

Inside the tower stairwell, Lyric bent over the railing, lungs burning with each ragged breath. She looked down through the gap between flights to witness State Police officers rushing upward, their movements synchronized and relentless.

She pushed onward, legs protesting as she reached the next landing. Her phone remained on, still clutched in her hand, speaker activated.

"Rada! It's Lyric! Call off your dogs!" Her voice cracked under the strain of fear and exertion.

Outside, sunlight glinted off the waxed surfaces of State Police cruisers as officers deployed around the tower's base. Car doors hung open, providing makeshift cover. One officer raised a bullhorn to his lips.

"Turn yourself in!" The amplified command reverberated against stone and glass.

Nearby, another officer knelt behind his vehicle door, rifle braced against the window frame, its barrel trained on the tower's upper reaches.

Inside, Lyric reached the final flight of stairs, legs trembling with fatigue. Above her, the empty belfry was bright from light that poured in through an arched window. The empty chamber offered no escape—a beautiful trap.

"Don't jump! Hands up!" The officers' voices merged into a wall of sound behind her, approaching from the stairs.

The State Police closed in, boots thundering against the steps. Desperate, Lyric clawed at the window frame, fingers searching for a latch, a crack, any means of escape. The light bathed her in gold as she turned to face her pursuers, arms raised.

"I am unarmed! I am unarmed!" The words tore from her throat.

"Put the phone down! Down, down!" Multiple voices commanded.

Slowly, deliberately, Lyric bent her knees, placing the phone on the steel floor. The call remained connected, speaker broadcasting every sound.

"Governor? Mira?! Please!" Desperation colored every syllable.

Her voice carried down the staircase as well, echoing through the structure until it reached the landing near the back door to the office. The landing where David, Mira,

Rada, and the Fixer's Assistant clustered, their faces upturned as they listened to the drama unfolding above.

"We're here!" Mira called back, tense with concern.

"What did you do?!" Rada demanded, confusion and anger warring in her.

"No-no-no. I have the killer with me!" David interrupted, words tumbling over each other. His grip on the Assistant's arm tightened as he attempted to shift blame. He set out to paint her and the Fixer in custody as the architects of everything gone wrong.

Their voices collided in the stairwell, accusations and denials rising and falling between the flights of stairs.

In the belfry, nausea rolled through Lyric's stomach as concern for the Assistant overwhelmed her.

"No! I know who the killer is! Mira — Rada, I printed proof!"

On the landing below, Governor Rada's face contorted as she struggled to piece together the competing claims. Behind her, Mira reacted visibly to the mention of "proof," regret flashing across her mouth as she remembered Lyric's print request. She slipped back through the office door, moving with renewed purpose.

"I'm innocent! Please listen," Lyric pleaded, her voice carrying down to them.

The Assistant wrenched herself free from David's crushing grip, her own eyes widening with realization.

"Let go!" The Assistant barked at David. "You said 'killer?' But..." The Assistant turned toward Rada, confusion contorting her youthful face. "*You* said 'attempted' assassination."

Trapped between versions of truth, Rada stepped forward, her political survival demanded an intervention.

"What do you want, Lyric!?" Her voice carried authority even in its uncertainty.

In the belfry, Lyric forced her breathing to slow, willing her voice to steadiness despite the guns trained on her.

"Let's talk. You, me, and David."

The State Police officers surrounding her maintained their positions, weapons unwavering, tension radiating from every rigid posture.

In the main bullpen, at the printers, Mira pulled papers from the output tray with frantic energy. A touch on her arm startled her—Estelle stood beside her, offering another stack of documents.

"Give her this too," Estelle said, her expression communicating volumes beyond the simple instruction.

Surprise registered on Mira's face, followed by gratitude. She clutched both sets of documents and ran toward the stairwell.

Seconds later, Lyric descended the clock tower stairs, hands secured before her with standard-issue restraints. State Police officers flanked her, their expressions professionally blank. As the group approached the landing outside the PAC office's back door, Mira emerged, papers in hand.

David pointed at the Fixer young Assistant.

"She's coming too," David insisted, voice tight with barely contained menace.

Mira held the freshly printed documents folded into a makeshift envelope. She caught Lyric's eye, offering a subtle nod toward the papers. Understanding passed between them in a fraction of a second.

"No press. No offense," Lyric stated, her tone firmer than her circumstances might suggest.

"Agreed," Rada responded, political self-preservation evident in her immediate acquiescence.

"She needs to come. It's vital," David pressed, drawing attention to himself and the Assistant.

In this moment of distraction, as all eyes focused on David's insistence, Mira executed a flawless handoff. The envelope passed from her fingers to Lyric's bound hands as the officers escorted her past. The papers disappeared into Lyric's grasp, unseen by anyone else.

SHOWDOWN

The heavy metal door to the building's basement creaked open. Governor Rada strode in ahead of her entourage. A few fluorescent lights buzzed above

"Who is this?" Rada demanded, her voice echoing against the hard surfaces.

The Fixer sat slumped in a folding metal chair against a partition of chain-link fence. His wrist hung awkwardly, secured to the chair with a handcuff. His face bore the marks of rough handling—a purpling bruise bloomed on his cheekbone, and a trickle of dried blood traced from his split lip. The man now appeared every one of his years.

David entered behind the Governor, his polished shoes clicking on the concrete floor. He moved with the confidence of someone who believed victory was imminent.

"This is the killer. An eco-terrorist—"

"I write for *The Post*," the Fixer interrupted, his voice hoarse but unwavering.

Rada pivoted, her gaze shifting to the young woman standing beside one of the State Troopers—the Assistant who had earlier been introduced to her as *The Post* journalist.

"Then who is she?" Rada asked, pointing.

The Fixer straightened, wincing at the pull of the handcuff against his wrist. "My assistant."

David stepped forward, his face flushed with righteous indignation. "No, your co-conspirator. You two infiltrated our campaign—"

He thrust the tote bag forward like a prosecutor presenting evidence. The words "Nevertheless, She Persisted" stood out boldly against the canvas.

"—and this is the proof. We found it in your car." David turned to the Fixer, jabbing a finger toward him. "She may have bought this, but you killed with it."

The Fixer strained against his restraint. "Horseshit—you crazy fascist."

The door swung open again as a State Trooper pushed Lyric into the room. David, agitated, pulled out a pistol from his pants. The metallic gleam of the weapon captured the light from above.

"Sir. Your weapon!! Down!" The State Cop's command cut through the tension.

David's mouth curved into a smirk. "It's not mine."

Governor Rada studied the gun with narrowed eyes, recognition dawning on her face. She gave a casual shrug, her shoulders rising and falling under her expensive suit jacket.

"It's mine. Relax."

Rada tilted her head, puzzlement creasing her brow as she struggled to reconcile who these people were. Her earlier understanding began to unravel. "So, wait a minute—"

"Ma'am. I'd rather—" The State Trooper began.

Rada held up one manicured hand. "Please."

The Trooper understood her command as stand down when really all she was asking for was a moment to figure out who was the real journalist. As the Trooper retreated to the corner of the room, Lyric seized the opportunity, stepping forward to derail Rada's train of thought.

"Rada. I have discovered the killer. Let me explain. Please. Madam Governor?"

The Governor's gaze moved between the pot-bellied Fixer and Lyric, confusion evident in her expression. Her eyes returned to the Fixer, scrutinizing him.

"So it is or it isn't him?"

David crossed his arms, smugness radiating from his stance as he addressed Lyric, caught in this pickle. "Let's hear it."

"I didn't do anything," the Fixer protested, his voice rising with frustration.

"Shut up," David snapped before turning to Lyric. "Well...?"

Lyric began her explanation with an exaggerated gesture of her cuffed hands, drawing deliberate attention to her restraints.

"Cal was murdered last night. By a jealous lover. Governor, you need to know my past."

She froze mid-gesture, staring at her bound hands as if noticing them for the first time.

"I mean... could you?" she asked, her voice softening. "It's really hard to talk like this. I mean..."

Her gaze shifted to Rada, eyes pleading. The Governor nodded to the Trooper, who stepped forward to unlock Lyric's cuffs. Once freed, she moved away from him, positioning herself in the center of the room like an actor taking stage.

"I used to be romantically involved with David. On a campaign, a kiss, it was a..." Lyric paused, directing a soft smile toward David, who remained unmoved.

"So what?" he challenged…while confirming her narrative.

"He has been after me for months. Emails, texts... I printed a few of the sexual innuendos, quid pro quo offers—harmless flirting perhaps, but I knew what I was getting into coming down here on an all-expense weekend."

David responded with a dismissive shrug, again granting credence to Lyric's framing.

"David even invited me to be with him at Hilton Head. Did you know he invited me to your vacation house?" Lyric continued, her gaze fixed on Rada.

The Governor's posture stiffened. She turned to David: "Is this true?"

Lyric handed over several printed pages, which Rada accepted with careful fingers.

"It's nothing," David insisted.

"Emails, texts—" Lyric began.

David cut her off, voice rising. "You were seen fleeing the scene of the crime!"

"No," Lyric countered, her voice steady. "I was stalked while on a date with Cal. Yes, I did go on a date with Cal. And yes, we had sex."

Rada flinched, a micro-expression of discomfort passing across her face.

"But David found out about me and Cal," Lyric continued, addressing Rada directly.

"Absurd!" David exclaimed.

"He's holding the murder weapon. And in there is my green coat he's been searching for ever since I had it—in Cal's room—thirteen."

Lyric's calm glance toward Rada carried a weight of unspoken meaning. The Governor's eyes widened slightly, her mind working through the implications.

"Interesting. In his room." Rada nodded.

David's composure cracked. "What are you doing? You tried to hide the coat!"

"I was seen on a date with Cal in it. I didn't want you to know about it. I was afraid you'd get jealous," Lyric explained before turning back to Rada. "Exactly like he did!"

"Why were you seen on the fire escape?" David demanded.

"Why were you stalking me?" Lyric pushed back at David. "It was you who saw me—" Lyric paused, letting the accusation hang in the air before turning toward Rada: "Because nobody else could have seen me."

David's voice rose to a near shout at Lyric. "This is ridiculous. Rada, you're not gonna go along with this! Are you?!"

Lyric stepped back, creating space for her narrative to unfold. Her voice grew stronger, more assured.

"You were here late at night, as always. And you went to Cal." Then in tones mocking his voice she added, "You carry the master key with you—"

"Not all the time—" David interjected, both to Lyric and Rada.

"—and you saw signs of our drunken date. He was passed out, so you took his unfinished whiskey bottle and you killed him with it."

David's laugh ricocheted off the concrete walls. "Oh my God. Hah!"

"Then you called... a car..."

Lyric rifled through her stack of papers, extracting one which she handed to Rada. Lyric remained before Rada, presenting the next set of points.

"This is a printout of our car service's records. The driver's name is Emory. He picked someone up at 1:30 AM and drove them to 206 Maggie Road. Who lives there?" She paused, eyes turning to lock with David's. "David, is where you live?"

"What are you doing?!" David exploded. Hurt welled up in his voice. He begged his boss: "Rada. Governor. Say something!"

Lyric found another document in her stack. She read aloud for Rada, her voice carrying an authoritative tone.

"Here's an email from Estelle, today, saying David deleted this building's security video." She glanced at a nearby Trooper. "To cover his tracks last night."

She turned to another page. "Here's a note... from Cal... to me..."

Her voice faltered, genuine emotion breaking through her composed facade. The paper trembled slightly in her hand. She had not yet seen anything that Mira salvaged from Cal's computer. This was one.

"A draft email. His ideas for a tell-all book..." She raised her eyes to Rada. "...about you. Ahem..." Lyric had to clear her throat and move past the emotions.

Lyric regained her composure, adopting a nonchalant tone as she addressed the Governor. "Now, I don't know what he's talking about—" Lyric tilted her head slightly. "I doubt there's anything to tell... Right?"

Lyric stepped away again and pointed at David. "But did David find out? That Cal wanted to create a scandal?"

She continued her rhetorical questioning, her voice rising and falling with rhetorical grace.

"But how would David even learn about this? Or about Cal and me? Simple: Cal's. Phone."

Lyric spoke into David's shocked face: "It wasn't with Cal when we found him. Nope." Then back to Rada Lyric spun more: "David already had it hidden in his safe. I'll bet it's still there?"

David's involuntary twitch confirmed her accusation without words.

"Of course it's there. Governor, you said David doesn't like loose ends."

Lyric gestured subtly toward the State Trooper. "I know that's two motives, but did David kill Cal for both reasons?" She turned fully to Rada. "Out of loyalty to you, or jealousy for me? Either way, David killed Cal."

She stepped aside, clearing a path between the Trooper and David. "Governor, direct this Officer to arrest David for suspected murder."

David huffed out a laugh, hollow and forced, while everyone else remained silent.

Duke, in the chair, smiled with uncontained amazement.

"Rada, I've been totally loyal to you, always. I have kept your secrets, I—"

"David," the Governor interrupted. "Your loyalty means everything."

Relief washed over his face. "Thank you."

"Absolutely everything," Rada continued, her tone shifting subtly. The room grew still as she recognized her opportunity for a scapegoat with witnesses present. "I swear to you, I am going to get you the best lawyer money can buy."

The color drained from David's face. "No! Goddamnit, Rada, no!"

His composure shattered completely. He ran a hand through his hair, tugging at it as his face flushed crimson with rage.

"I promise leniency—" Rada began.

"Gun down," the State Trooper ordered, his own weapon now drawn.

"Rada! What the fuck?!" David screamed.

"Put the gun DOWN!!" the Trooper commanded again.

David seemed deaf to everything around him. His face darkened to a deep red as he took a small step toward the Governor, desperation radiating from every pore.

"The Party! The White House!!!"

"Don't move!" the Trooper barked.

David spun toward Lyric, the pistol still raised too high.

"God damn you! Fucking bit—"

BANG! BANG! BANG!

The Trooper's shots exploded through the confined space, striking David's chest in rapid succession. The reports reverberated off the concrete walls, amplifying the violence.

David crumpled backward, dead before he hit the floor.

Pain seared through Lyric and Rada's ears from the thunderous gunshots. The Fixer, equally deafened, watched in stunned silence.

Lyric forced her eyes open, drawing in a ragged breath. Her lungs heaved as if she'd been holding her breath underwater.

More State Troopers burst into the cellar, weapons drawn, their boots pounding on the concrete.

"Clear. Clear," one called out.

Officers rushed forward, ushering the Assistant and the Governor out of the room, away from the spreading pool of crimson beside David's body. He lay flat on his back, eyes fixed on the ceiling, seeing nothing.

Lyric blinked, long and hard. When her eyes opened again, her breath shuddered in her chest, the tremor of it shaking through her entire body. It was over.

***

The evening lights of the main bullpen were on casting a sallow glow across drawn faces. A somber quiet hung in the air, the kind which follows in the wake of chaos. Lyric stood outside Governor Rada's closed office door, arms wrapped around petite Mira. The smaller woman's frame trembled against hers.

The heavy oak door to Rada's office swung open. State Police officers filed out one by one, their expressions professionally blank, giving nothing away. Their boots clomped against the floor as they dispersed into the bullpen.

"What's happening?" Mira stepped forward, her voice small yet insistent.

One of the officers—a broad-shouldered man with a regulation haircut and tired eyes—paused in his stride.

"Investigation's over." Two words, flat and definitive, falling into the space between them like stones.

After the procession of officers cleared, Governor Rada appeared in her doorway. Her posture remained rigid despite the hours of tension, not a crease in her suit or a hair out of place. She beckoned to Lyric with a subtle nod, an invitation into her office.

Mira squeezed Lyric's hand—a wordless communication, part reassurance, part warning. The pressure of her fingers spoke volumes: *Be careful. Stay sharp.* Lyric returned the gesture and stepped across the threshold.

When Governor Rada closed the door with a soft click, Lyric had already claimed a power spot on the front edge of Rada's desk, her posture deliberately casual. A nonchalance masking the coiled tension beneath.

"What's next?" Lyric asked, her tone inscrutable.

Rada moved toward her desk with composure. "When the Captain returns he'll write up a report."

"Hm. No." Lyric shook her head, a sharp little movement. "I mean what's next for you?"

A smile spread across Rada's face—the smile of a victor savoring triumph. She lowered herself onto a leather chair, limbs pouring over the arms in relaxed confidence, claiming space as only the truly powerful do.

"I am the front runner. The sympathy from this is gonna be...just..." Her words trailed off, her imagination clearly painting glorious futures in her mind's eye.

Lyric blinked, genuinely taken aback by the depth of Rada's self-delusion. The governor existed in a reality entirely of her own making, one where consequences were for other people.

"I only wish it came closer to the Convention," Rada continued, lost in her fantasy of power.

"I'm gonna pass on the job." Lyric delivered the words without inflection.

Rada leaned forward, enthusiasm undimmed. "Run the campaign! What if you start your strategy firm?! Let this be your first client. I will set you up for life. Wasn't that David's big idea?"

At the mention of David's name, something shifted in Lyric's expression. She took her time responding, swallowing against the tightness in her throat as her mind wandered to another absence.

"...Cal..." The name emerged as barely more than a whisper.

Lyric clenched her jaw, refusing to surrender to grief in Rada's presence. She bit down hard on the inside of her cheek, tasting copper, using physical pain to combat emotional vulnerability.

"Great sadness," Rada acknowledged with political precision, neither too dismissive nor too affected. "And we keep everything between us?"

"You, me, and Emory." Lyric watched Rada's face intently.

"Who?" Genuine confusion creased Rada's brow.

Lyric seethed: "Your driver." Lyric leaned forward slightly. "What's the Captain's report gonna say...about Emory?"

"Ah, he drowned on vacation." Rada delivered the line with practiced ease.

"In Bermuda." Lyric's words hung in the air between them.

The implications had not yet registered with Rada. Her face remained composed, untroubled by the undercurrents of what Lyric had revealed.

"Your run..." Lyric stood from the desk, her posture straightening. "...is over."

She strode past Rada without a backward glance, pulling the door open and stepping through it with the decisive movement of someone closing a chapter forever.

Lyric emerged from Rada's office, her hand slipped into her pocket, extracting her phone with practiced ease. Her thumb pressed against the screen, stopping the audio recording app with a soft beep.

Mira waited nearby, eyes widening with unspoken questions. Lyric grabbed her hand, fingers interlacing, and pulled her forward into motion.

"We have to go. Now." The urgency in Lyric's voice was clear.

They hurried past a table laden with evidence, bags and documents spread across its surface like artifacts from another life. The battered tote bag remained there, its familiar slogan still visible through smudges and wear: "Nevertheless, She Persisted." The words carried a new weight now, an unintended prophecy fulfilled.

***

The Washington Journal's offices pulsed with the constant rhythm of a newsroom—phones ringing, keyboards clacking, voices rising and falling on phone calls. In a glass-walled office at the heart of this organized chaos, Lyric's editor Tae-sung Lee shot up from his chair as if propelled by springs. His phone instantly pressed against his ear.

"Holy shit what happened?!" His voice carried both concern and professional excitement—the hallmarks of a career journalist confronted with breaking news.

The hybrid hatchback sped along I-95 through traffic. Inside, the atmosphere hung heavy with unspoken thoughts and lingering adrenaline. Lyric sat in the backseat beside Mira, shoulders slumped with the weight of recent events. Through the windshield, the blur of forest slid past on their northbound trajectory.

"It's a long story. We're safe...ish." Exhaustion tinged every syllable of Lyric's response.

In the front seat, the Fixer exchanged a grateful glance with his Assistant.

"You'll need to bring your Fed friend." Lyric's voice carried both resignation and resolution.

***

Sunlight danced across the turquoise waters of Bermuda's Great Sound, a perfect postcard scene. Near a private dock, water lapped against wooden pilings, toying with a loose rope—physical evidence of absence. The small rowboat Lyric had spoken of had vanished.

Up the manicured lawn, framed by exotic flowers, the State Trooper Captain emerged from the mansion's grand French doors. His uniform remained crisp despite the humid air, his stride purposeful as he descended toward the water. Behind him followed the scurrying Housekeeper and a young Security guard, their postures apologetic, hands gesturing in explanation.

The Captain halted at the empty dock, his gaze scanning the horizon before dropping in evident frustration. His jaw clenched beneath a professionally neutral expression.

The island Housekeeper stepped forward, her words lilting with the musical cadence of the local dialect. "He rowed a boat out, then got on a big boat, then they gone away."

The Captain's glare silenced any further explanations. He reached for his phone, one button to call HQ. He waited, dreading the conversation to come. Bad news traveled poorly across oceans, especially when headed toward someone like Governor Rada Waylos.

Sunset painted the Potomac River in hues of pink and violet, the water's surface caught and scattered the colors of the sunset clouds. A yacht cut through this splendor, its white hull gleaming as it approached Columbia Island Marina in Arlington, Virginia.

On the ship's foredeck, passengers gathered to witness their arrival. Among them stood Emory, a young African American man whose last few whirlwind days had, perhaps unbeknownst to him, brought him quite near to death. His eyes scanned the shoreline, brightening when they landed on a familiar figure. His wave carried the enthusiasm of someone granted an unexpected second chance. Surely, he had unpuzzled the sinister purpose of his "vacation."

On shore, petite Mira returned the gesture with equal vigor, her Lebanese heritage evident in her olive complexion and dark curls.

Beside her stood Lyric, summoning a smile that didn't quite reach her eyes.

The Fixer and his Assistant flanked them, alongside Tae-sung and his Federal Agent boyfriend, the latter's impeccable suit standing out in the natural setting.

The Fed broke away from the group, crossing the grass to Lyric. He extended his card to her with professional courtesy - a smile of appreciation on his face.

"Your audio file makes our case." The words carried official gratitude, but Lyric received them without joy.

Her expression remained downcast, shoulders bearing invisible weight. She grappled with guilt as tangible as any physical burden—grief at her role in David's downfall, regardless of its necessity. The Fed guided her away from the others, toward the water's edge where conversation could remain private.

"You made the right call. ...Hey." He waited until Lyric refocused, her eyes meeting his. "You saved lives. And for what it's worth, I think you're a born PI."

Surprise flashed across Lyric's features, genuine and unguarded. Before she could respond, Tae approached, having caught fragments of their exchange.

"She's got a job, thanks." His possessive tone was wrapped in humor.

"Not with you. No offense." Lyric almost smiled, the corner of her mouth twitching upward before remorse transformed the expression into something more complicated.

Mira darted past them, her hand squeezing Lyric's shoulder in joy. "Look what you did—he's okay!"

She bounded toward the dock where Emory now disembarked from the yacht, solid ground beneath his feet for the first time in days.

Lyric followed at an unhurried pace, allowing distance to form between herself and Mira – however closely Mira knew Emory, Lyric wanted to give them a moment of privacy. Tae and the Fed remained behind, their own conversation continuing without her.

The Fixer fell into step beside her, his words low and meant for her ears alone. "Lyric. You need to finish his book."

"Cal?" The name emerged as a question though she knew the answer.

"Yeah. Yours and Cal's. Can you write?"

Lyric paused mid-stride, considering. Something shifted in her expression—purpose forming from grief's ashes.

"Yes. I can. Yeah. And I'm good."

Behind the welcome party, above the canopy of trees, the towering Washington Monument stood as a silent witness to the majesty of America's Capital. Its obelisk silhouetted against the warm glowing colors of the sunset's peak. All the pollution of the westward land catching the setting sun was almost inspiring. Almost.